MW01135724

RISE *of the*
SEVEN

RISE *of the* SEVEN

MELISSA WRIGHT

Cover art by Gene Mollica Studio

Book design by Maureen Cutajar
www.gopublished.com

ISBN-13: 978-1482340112
ISBN-10: 1482340119

Special thanks to Annie,
who helped bring Freya to life.

MOLLY

Small lines of text curled deliciously around the page, leading through a decadent city, a torturous romance, a wicked betrayal. Molly's hand traced the intricate pattern of runes that interlaced and surrounded the illustration of the temptress, Floret Shade, and she became distracted from her reading, studying the fairy's long golden hair that seemed to float on the wind and mingle with the folds of her gown. Such a rich gown, beaded in an impossibly complex design that one would likely never even notice, considering how the bodice, cinched unfeasibly tight, presented her bosom. And, as if the display were not enough, the pale skin was dappled with droplets of jewels that glistened in the twilight, ensuring her prey would be ensnared. Molly sighed as she rolled over, hopelessly yearning for that sort of strength and beauty.

She felt the cool grass beneath her skin and became aware once more of the passage of time. It was nearing dark and if she didn't return quickly, her father would skin her. She tucked the book into her satchel and hiked up her skirt to run through the tall grass.

"Molly Mayanne!"

Her father's sharp tone cut through her daydreams of fairies and she froze, forgetting for a good half minute to drop her skirt back down. He stared at her.

"Father." She struggled for a moment, deciding whether to come up with some sort of explanation. But she couldn't know if he was angry about the late hour or something else she'd done—or forgotten to do. She settled on a brief, "Hi," and a smile.

It was the wrong choice.

He grabbed her arm to haul her back toward the village, chastising her the entire way about wasting time on foolish tales of fairies and magic when there was work to be done. She hoped he didn't see her roll her eyes, but after a few more steps, her temper got the best of her. She jerked her arm free and glared at him. "I am certain you don't intend to let the neighbors see you treat me this way," she spat as she stomped the remainder of the way back.

He followed her and shut the door behind them before starting up again. "Molly, a young woman cannot be traipsing around the forest. A lady must protect her virtue."

She snickered; her virtue had been lost long ago, when she was but six and ten, to handsome John Black under the shade of the heart tree.

The apparent lightheartedness infuriated her father. "Molly, it is time to choose a husband."

She bit down hard against the words that would come and he saw her defiance.

"*Past* time."

The insult stung and she stewed for a long while after he left her alone in the cabin. And then, eventually, she began to prepare their dinner. Her mind wandered from the resentment at her situation to the options available to her. Joseph Black, John's older brother, was a farmer and she imagined herself in a muck-smeared apron, carrying slop to the pigs or on her hands and knees tending the crops. Or James Black, their cousin, who earned his living hunting and trapping. Would he expect her to skin and tan hides? She'd missed her chance with John—he'd long since married another, as he seemed unable to forgive her for kissing one of the Baker boys. She couldn't even consider the preacher, who'd made his interest in her quite plain, without giggling. No, she couldn't see herself with any of them. And that was how she'd ended up without a husband so late in her years. She wanted more.

When her father returned late, he seemed in unusually high spirits—especially given that Molly had allowed his dinner to get cold. As he sat at the table, she eyed him suspiciously from her chair in the corner of the room. She would have dismissed herself to her room, but she was in the middle of the tale of Bonnie Bell and, no matter how often she'd read it, the story made her skin crawl. Her father finished his meal and stood, humming a cheery tune as he carried his dish to the basin, dipped it in, wiped it dry, and returned it to its place on the shelf. Molly sat up.

When he spun, a grin sneaked across his face. "No," she declared immediately.

He threw up his hands and all mirth dropped from his features. "Molly, there is no reason—"

"No." She crossed her arms as defiantly as she could manage.

"Are you not even curious——"

"Fine." She stopped him again. "Who?"

He sighed and settled back into a chair, bracing himself with a forearm on the table. "Jackson Redding."

Her gasp of horror shut him down a third time. Jackson was more than ten years her senior, and those years had not been kind. She knew her father would not allow her dismissal on such vain grounds, so, heated, she chose another argument. "He's married thrice."

"He is widowed," her father insisted, "and you would be his third wife."

"The third to die and make him a widower again," she shot back. "Is that how you would see me?"

He stood to face her. "I would see you married before my years are over and no one remains to care for my only daughter." His declaration deflated her and she stared at the floor as he continued, "Jackson has made an upstanding offer and I urge you to consider it."

She didn't respond and, after a moment, he went to his room. She felt guilty, and relieved the conversation was over, and distraught about the entire matter, until she heard him stop just outside his door. She froze.

"And if you refuse the offer," he said, "you will inform him yourself."

The next morning, guilt had her up early. She hated spending long days inside, sewing and mending and such, so she pulled down a basket and headed out to pick berries.

As often happened when she set out with good intentions, she ended up lying on the creek bank, perusing the collection of fairy tales, empty basket at hand. Her father had advised her that by simply leaving the book at home she could avoid such issues, but she'd thought him ridiculous. She would never abandon something of such importance; she carried it with her everywhere, even sewing a hidden pocket in the back of her gown. It had been aged when she'd found it and though she endeavored to keep it well, the pages were tattered and worn.

She had drifted from those pages, imagining a life among the magic and dreams told within, when a sharp sound pulled her from her reverie.

She glanced around but couldn't determine what it was because of the babble of the creek. She stood, narrowing her eyes at a motion a short distance away, and followed the sound, leaving her basket and book in the grass. As she approached the dark mass, its movement increased and she could see that it was a small animal, frantic now at her advance. It seemed to be caught among some weeds and abandoned fishing lines near a shallow on the other side of the creek. She stepped closer to the bank and leaned forward, trying to judge the depth. There was no way she could cross at that point, but she was fairly certain there was a rocky area a little farther down. She'd never crossed there, she wasn't even allowed to be this far out.

The ball of fur whined and she realized it was a pup.

Excited now, she ran down the bank, searching for the rocks, worrying the entire way whether the pup had been abandoned by his mother, if there were more pups, whether her father would allow a mutt to run in the village.

When she saw the rocks, she leapt in, not bothering with searching for the best path. She splashed across and nearly fell, but managed to only soak the hem of her skirt. When she reached the far bank, the pup called out again and she was off.

He shuddered and yowled as she came close and Molly put her hands up in a calming gesture as she slowly stepped forward. It was too much. He struggled free of the tangle. She went after him, aiming to grab his body from behind, but he was fast and her boots were slick. She slipped twice and muddied her skirt and apron before righting herself and starting again.

They ran and ran. The poor little fur ball was exhausted and he finally gave, dropping onto the fallen leaves with an exaggerated sigh. Molly approached this time in a lowered stance, crawling the last few feet. She crouched and watched him for a long while. When his breathing finally slowed, she leaned forward to her knees and then her belly as she lay on the forest floor beside him and reached out tentatively to touch him.

He was so soft. She was amazed by the feel of him and took to petting the silky fluff, cringing at the few bald spots he'd created by tearing free. She cooed, and it only took a moment before he warmed to her, nuzzling his little black nose against her arm and inching closer.

They lay in the shadow of the trees for some time, until the pup became restless again and began to whine. Even covered as he was in fluff, she could feel the bones of his ribs, the narrowness of his stomach. Slowly, she stood, taking him in her arms to carry him home, regardless of her father's likely reaction.

It only took three steps to realize she didn't know which way was home. She hadn't noticed how far they'd come in the chase, so far that she'd lost the sound of the creek. She glanced around and, clutching the pup to her chest, headed toward what appeared to be an opening in the canopy of trees. If she could get out of the forest, she could find the creek and her path.

But when she reached the clearing, she was encircled by trees. She narrowed her eyes, a challenge to the dark forest, and headed back in, determined to find her way home.

Nearly an hour later, she realized someone was following her.

It had crept up on her, that feeling of being watched, that sensitivity to the softest noises at her every turn. She slowed, forcing herself to only glance back momentarily, not to run. There was nothing there but trees and shadows. She breathed deep as she turned to continue, and then froze.

Standing casually in her path was the most terrifying, beautiful... *creature* in existence. He could not but be a creature, for he was no man.

Riven stood before the human girl, waiting for the instinct of flight to kick in. He looked her over as she stared back at him. Her skirts were caked with mud, her hair a tangled mess. *Filthy humans*, he thought as he tried to estimate her age. No more than one and twenty, he was fairly certain, old enough for breeding stock at any rate. She was thin, but her hips appeared adequate, bosom sufficient. *Well enough*, he decided. As his eyes returned to her face, he took in her expression, saw the coy smile, the flush of her skin. She was flirting with him.

She lowered the animal she held to her waist, presenting herself more fully. He closed the distance, grabbed her arm and yanked her toward him. Her face contorted only a moment before smoothing as she pressed into him. He recoiled, moving her back by her upper arm.

She glared at him, finally understanding her advance was unwanted. "Well, you're the one gaping at me," she huffed, indicating her chest with a glance.

He stared at her, baffled, as she struggled to release his grip. He had never understood these creatures, but this one might have been the oddest of the lot.

"Remove. Your. Hand," she demanded firmly.

"Calm yourself," he instructed in as even a tone as he could manage. She did just that, crossing her arms and slanting a hip. It seemed surprising she had accomplished the posture, given that one arm was solidly in his grip and the other held a young dog.

She raised her brow, questioning and challenging.

He allowed himself a small nod; she would do just fine. There was no doubt Lord Asher would be pleased.

And Asher had been pleased. The girl had not even required persuasion. It seemed she took in everything, understood the whole of it, and accepted her place in the matter. The only emotion appeared to be pride as she gladly received the honor a king offered to bestow on her.

It was effected quickly and before the next moon they were crossing the hidden passages again, Riven, the blissful human girl, and her unborn child. They rode for days, stopping often in consideration of the fragile condition of the girl.

Riven nearly smirked at the thought, knowing full well her condition wasn't the concern. His lord had wanted this child above all others, certain the girl's stubbornness and bizarre outlook were somehow a sign of what she would produce. Had Riven any question about the idea, it was quashed by his orders to hide her in their most secure location.

He was a faithful warrior; he had never challenged his king. But this commission was testing him.

"And he will be strong," Molly carried on, her posture so different from that of the girl he'd found in the southern forests. Her tone was haughty, as if she'd been born crowned. "I'm certain his eyes will be hazel, as my father's are."

Riven scanned the clearing, using all of his senses in the search.

"Ah, my father," she continued, "he has no idea of my good fortune. I have often wondered what transpired there after I left. Had the villagers searched far enough, they would have found the muddy prints on the far bank." She paused, likely reconsidering their reaction. She'd maintained they would be convinced she had run off after her father's demand that she marry. That she didn't relish the thought of him in pain. She forced a laugh. "No, I'm certain they found my book of tales and decided the fairies spirited me away."

Her hand fluttered in the air and Riven resisted the urge to break her fingers.

They stopped and Riven dismounted his horse, pulling his pack with him. Molly stared at him until he assisted her down from her own. When he pulled her pack down as well, he snapped a command at the horses and they crossed the clearing in a trot, then disappeared into the trees.

"Why did you do that?" she demanded.

"We continue from here on foot."

Molly's mouth fell open in shock, but she quickly schooled her features. *Not long*, she thought, *not long and I will be treated as a queen.* She unwrapped the shoulder sling at her side and helped the small pup down for some exercise. She'd not given him much attention over the last weeks, though he'd been her only real companion. The elves seemed pleased to have her, but they weren't exactly sociable. Until she had her child, the pup was her only source of true loyalty.

When she looked up, Riven threw her a hunk of dried meat. The pup bounced excitedly, so she slid it into a waist pocket to eat later, when she could discreetly share with him.

Without a word, Riven began walking. Molly picked up the pup, wrestled him back into his carrier, and pressed her forearm against the bag to settle him as she hurried to catch up.

Riven had a long stride.

They walked for nearly an hour before the exertion began to be too much for Molly. She pushed the hood of her cloak back and the chill breeze prickled the damp skin of her neck. She tilted her head back and fanned the material of her blouse to let the wind reach more skin.

The sky was beautiful, blue and endless. A hawk circled lazily, far above them. Molly stumbled on a rock and brought her eyes back to the ground to watch her footing. Riven hadn't seemed to notice, but the pup at her side groaned at the disturbance of his nap.

A dull thump sounded a short distance to her right, but before she had a chance to look, she walked into Riven's back. He'd stopped in his tracks; he was looking toward the noise. Molly's eyes followed his, her head cocked to one side as she realized it was the hawk. It had fallen out of the sky.

Suddenly, she was jerked off her feet as Riven began to run. He had a death grip on her; she wasn't able to look behind them. When she looked forward, there was nothing but a tree line in the distance. She had no idea where they were going, what was happening, but Riven's reaction spiked unadulterated fear in her.

And then he stopped running. His chest heaved as he dropped Molly to her feet beside him. He released his grip on her but she stood, frozen. Riven stared on as they were descended upon, his arms and shoulders braced.

The first to approach were ethereal, tall and thin, silvery robes beneath their cloaks. Molly stared at them in awe. They stopped several feet away and spoke to Riven. But Molly couldn't focus on their words because she'd seen two wolves in the distance. Great beasts.

There was a commotion in front of her, low, angry words, and she turned back to find more elves confronting Riven. The newest arrivals were warrior-like, with the same otherworldly beauty as Riven. Dark hair and eyes, strong, muscular builds. She might have mistaken them for more of Asher's guard, except she'd seen no other address Riven as they did now.

Two cold words escaped one particularly large elf and she meant to focus on him, but Riven had dropped beside her. Her eyes fell to him, but there was nothing but a lumpy pile of material where he'd stood.

His cloak.

Face ashen, mouth agape, she looked back to the gathered mob, suddenly certain of her doom. Their grim expressions reinforced that theory and she swallowed hard, eyes wide. She felt the breeze hit her skin one last time.

"Stop!"

For a moment, Molly thought the voice was her own. But it wasn't. She found the source of the command, staring back at her with the same shocked, fearful expression she wore herself.

She was a small, striking woman, but mirrored Molly in only age and stature. Her hair was dark, her eyes lush green. There was something about her that wasn't quite human, Molly thought. And then Molly realized the force with which the very large, very strong elf was holding the woman back. He stared down at the dark beauty, his jaw was tight. He nearly seemed to be in pain. He nodded and Molly recognized it as a command to one of the other elves. She steadied herself for her fate. The breeze picked up again, a gust of wind hitting her square in the face, stealing her last breath.

She thought she heard a whispered, "No," as she closed her eyes.

Nothing happened. It might have only been moments—she'd lost all track of time since Riven had started running—but she opened her eyes to find the pair again. His eyes searched the woman's face, and she seemed to be asking him for something. Begging.

After a long instant, he turned from the woman, expression hard, and gestured to one of the others. Calling off the order.

Molly gasped in air, her knees weak, her hands trembling. Her frantic gaze fell back to the woman just in time to see her flushed skin go pale, her eyes roll back into her head. Dimly, she recognized the woman was having a seizure, or maybe fainting, and thought the same might come of her shortly. She lowered herself to the ground, shaking, but couldn't keep her eyes off the band of elves. They surrounded the woman. A wild redhead and the elf who had held her back earlier were holding the woman, easing her quaking body to the ground. *No, definitely not fainting*, Molly thought. The redhead looked worried, but the other, the elf whose expression had been so severe before, his face melted into pain as he stared at the woman. He pulled her from the redhead, cradling her trembling body in his arms to calm her. It was a restraint. It was an embrace.

Molly's breath hitched. She realized she was sobbing.

She realized she was alive.

It was some time before Molly's brain began to operate properly again. She knew she had been moved, she was aware of the goings-on around her, but the passage of time had become fuzzy.

When she'd rested, been settled onto a blanket, been given a canteen, that was when things started to clear up again. She couldn't say it was a sense of security. After weeks with Asher's guard, she wasn't that naive. But she didn't think this group planned to kill her. Not immediately, anyway.

The elves had assembled a camp, built a fire, and paced around. A lot. Molly had been watching them without realizing she'd been doing so, slowly grasping what was happening around her. The tall, white-haired elves were no longer in the camp. The rest, the large, frightening one, the wiry one who seemed to be always moving, and the handsome, cheerful one, appeared to be doing what Molly's father had called "busy work." The other handsome, definitely not cheerful one and the redhead were sitting by the dark-haired woman, who had yet to recover. Those two had barely spared Molly a glance, except when the redhead occasionally shot her an accusatory glance, though Molly couldn't understand exactly what she was being accused of.

She knew they'd killed one of Asher's head guards. She hadn't dared to let on her purpose, why she'd been with Riven, or that it had been voluntary. But they hadn't asked, either. In fact, they had barely spoken to her at all.

A grumbled complaint came from the bundle at Molly's side. She pulled the last of the dried meat from her pocket and slid it toward the pouch. The pup's head poked out and he anxiously sniffed until he located the source in Molly's hand.

She started when someone approached her. She looked up from her spot on the blanket to see a tall, handsome elf. The cheerful one.

As he stared down at her, or rather at her pup, Molly realized maybe cheerful had been a stretch. He was indeed smiling, but a slow, sexy smile. She glanced quickly to the other handsome one, the one watching the dark-haired woman, and decided she'd have to stick with Cheerful and Not Cheerful, as both were exceedingly, unnaturally, attractive. The group spoke little and had yet to call each other by name. She wasn't about to ask.

A low laugh escaped the elf beside her and her eyes automatically returned to him. She would have to try to quit gawking.

He lowered himself to squat, and reached out to run a hand over the pup's head. This caused the young dog to feign back and then bounce excitedly. He was playing with her pup. A nervous laugh bubbled up from Molly's chest and she nearly choked on it.

"What do you call him?" The elf's eyes connected with her own as he spoke and she lost her voice, her breath, for a moment.

"I... Uh, I don't have... Haven't named him yet." There. She'd gotten it out. She'd been in the company of elves for weeks, had grown accustomed to at least those of Asher's guard who didn't outwardly show their distaste toward her, but she'd been certain this new group would cut her down as they had Riven. It had taken a toll on her confidence.

Cheerful was watching her. His smile had the slightest twist to it, just one side, and she wondered if he was amused. "Well, it seems he should have a name. Don't you think?"

Molly nodded, still not quite able to return a grin.

"We shall work on that," he said.

She decided that did not sound like something someone would say if they were planning to kill her, and the tension in her chest released with a long sigh.

He noticed. But, before he had a chance to comment, Molly's attention was drawn once more across the camp to the other woman.

Molly realized then that she'd heard Not Cheerful and the redhead talking to the dark-haired woman in low tones since Cheerful had settled beside her. Since the others had stationed themselves closer to her. The woman had woken and, apparently, wasn't very happy about something. There was a bit of commotion, and then, suddenly, the redhead had a hold of the woman's wrists as she and Not Cheerful glared at each other. At this point, Molly considered renaming Not Cheerful "Murderous Rage."

Cheerful cleared his throat, a decidedly un-elf-like noise from what Molly had gathered, and spoke again, as if to distract her. "He will be quite large," he said, raising one of the puppy's heavy paws. Molly had noticed this before, as well as the dog's ravenous appetite. When his paw was released, the pup lifted both again in an attempt to regain the elf's attention. Cheerful rolled easily to his hip, kicking a bent leg out and leaning over to an elbow beside the pup, who took this action as a great victory and leapt toward the elf's outstretched hand for more play.

Molly laughed, familiar with the pup's antics.

"How does Rollo fit?" Cheerful asked, almost to himself. "No, no. Fredrik."

Molly scrunched her nose.

Cheerful laughed. "Not Fredrik, then. Dranson?"

The pup snuffed, as if he held great disdain for the name.

He tried again. "Flufferby?"

"That's ridiculous," Molly giggled.

He smiled. "You should call him Giggles, he seems to have that effect on you."

She shook her head, deciding to play his game. "Snickers."

The elf smirked and she suddenly had the oddest suspicion. None of the elves she'd met had been so casual. And here he sat, creating silly names for her pet. Not even asking her name. Not giving his own. Not any of theirs.

She looked toward the others. Something about each of them seemed to push Molly's gaze to fall on the woman. The woman with constant protectors. It reminded her of Asher. His guard.

The next day, the group was quiet as they departed camp. The horse Molly had been given was calm and steady, so, though she hadn't spent much time ahorse, she was able to relax and take in her surroundings. She didn't recognize anything. The ground was damp, but too peppered with rock to be muddy. The air was chill, the mountain looming behind them, black and ominous. A heavy fog hung near its top, clouding the sun and adding to the air of threat. Molly pulled her cloak tighter around her and shifted the pouch to cradle the pup in front of her.

She realized the wiry elf was watching her. Being watched wasn't unusual for her as of late, but it was generally Cheerful, not the others, none of whom seemed to like her. At all. She looked back at the elf for a moment. He was lean and handsome, an inexplicable quickness about him, even in stillness. His skin was flawless, his eyes as dark and rich as the bark of the roca pine. He wore a wary expression, saturated with distaste, and Molly averted her gaze. She knew he had an easy smile, she'd seen it. But it was only for the redhead.

Cheerful rode up beside Molly just then, acknowledging her with a nod. She beamed back at him. She couldn't help it.

He appeared to bite back a smirk. "Are you faring well with the mount?"

"Oh, yes," Molly gushed. "He is a handsome steed. My father would pay a pretty coin for such a stud."

Abruptly, Wiry choked on a laugh and kicked his horse to a faster pace. Molly looked to Cheerful, who seemed to be openly laughing at her. She didn't appreciate being made fun of, though she had no idea what she'd said wrong. And the memory of her father caused a stab of guilt. With this, her feathers were ruffled and she purposely guided her horse away from Cheerful, impatiently willing Asher to finally come for her. For his child.

It was the one thing she clung to. He would come for her. He had to come for her.

And then, early one evening, things changed. They had stopped well before nightfall, as they often did, to make camp. Molly had a suspicion the group was worried about the dark-haired woman. She seemed to need so much rest, she seemed… unwell. Not that she looked it. Truth be told, Molly was quite envious of her unnatural beauty. But there was something not quite right about her. And the others hovered around her, as if they expected a catastrophe at any moment. The woman didn't appear exactly graceless to Molly, but in comparison to the agility of their company, she might understand their concern.

The woman sat across the fire from them, and, as usual, Cheerful settled in beside Molly, angled between her and the others. As a general rule, Molly tried to avoid looking directly at the woman. But, every now and again, she caught sight of her face and recognized some of her own emotion there. A fierce determination. A confidence that belied her size. Only this woman carried more. Behind her eyes was chaos and fury.

The redhead noticed Molly's attention had fallen on the woman and intervened. She stepped before the fire, circling the rising flame as she spoke. She told of fairies, great tales of wondrous places, and Molly was mesmerized.

Every eye was on the redhead, and she clearly relished the attention. Her gaze fell in succession to each in her audience as she moved, a clink of metal, a wisp of material accenting every passage. The fire licked at the air behind her, as if dancing to the melody of her words, as if even the flames were entranced by her story.

Molly was enchanted, the yarn a dull thrum as her gaze fixed on the blaze. Sudden raucous laughter broke her trance, and she blinked, her eyes dry. Coming back to herself, she glanced around again at the elves.

Cheerful was watching her. He smiled, and this time Molly could believe it was genuine.

"She has a way with words," he said.

"Yes," Molly sighed. Her eyes roamed the camp again, in wonder at the world she had stepped into. A world right out of her books. A world to which she had only dreamed of belonging. Her gaze fell on the dark-haired woman, and she considered what her role could be in all of this. She clearly mattered to the group. Could there be some reason other than her own purpose for being involved?

"And where's your pup, sunshine?"

Molly smiled at Cheerful before starting to turn back to her contemplation of the woman. She jumped when he reached for her.

He leaned in as he tucked a strand of hair behind her ear, whispering conspiratorially. "Don't see much blonde around here."

For the first time in years, Molly blushed.

And then the fire exploded. For a moment, Molly thought the dark-haired woman was burning, that the explosion had thrown flames onto her. But, as everyone in the camp stared at the woman, waiting, Molly realized it was nothing of the sort.

Molly's mouth opened for a moment, closed, opened as she struggled for words. The woman. Flames had burst from her hands. She was unharmed by them. The woman had magic.

She was no mere woman, Molly realized, staring after the dark beauty as she and her male companion walked from the camp. When they were nearly out of sight, Molly turned to

Cheerful, who was still watching the couple. She couldn't quite make out the emotion on his face, but he seemed to snap out of it, suddenly turning to Molly. She knew the questions were clear in her expression, and she saw the same signs of displeasure appear on Cheerful's face that her father had worn in all the years since she'd turned eight. It made her smile.

Something in his eyes gave her the courage to ask her questions. "She isn't human."

He stiffened slightly, answer enough for Molly.

"You protect her," she continued.

Without warning, the largest of the elves was standing in front of them, the abrupt halt of his boots throwing chunks of dirt onto Molly's blanket and skirt. She looked up uneasily to find he was staring not at her, but at Cheerful. He stood, and Molly found herself staring up at them, Cheerful's frame dwarfed by this massive one. She felt a tingle run up her arms.

And then the wiry one was there. "We should discuss this elsewhere, I believe."

Molly was momentarily lost. She'd not seen a discussion. The giant didn't spare a look at her before turning from Cheerful and leaving the camp with Wiry.

Molly watched them. They were heading in the direction of the dark-haired woman and the other, the one who, no matter where he stood, watched the woman. The one who wore the tortured expression each time she slept. Her watcher. Her protector.

Yes, Molly thought, *this will be what awaits my son. He will be powerful. He will be protected. He will rule.*

The idea stopped Molly cold. Why were they protecting this woman? Asher was the ruler of the North. He had told her so himself. These elves had killed Riven. Asher's guard. And they surrounded this woman as if she were a treasure of highest consequence.

At first sight, Molly had almost thought the woman human. But she wasn't. She had magic.

She had a guard.

Molly started when Cheerful spoke beside her and she had to tuck away the implications for later. "Pardon?"

"Dinner," he repeated, gesturing with a small hunk of meat.

The pup launched himself toward it, quick as a whip, but too slow for the reflexes of an elf. Molly laughed, not only at the attempt, but the absurdity of her situation.

"Yes," Cheerful said, "Snickers is an apt name for the tiny beast."

They sat in companionable silence as they ate, and the others returned. The woman was rubbing circles on her temples, her gaze trailing the ground. Molly stole the opportunity to examine her face.

Molly would have said her features were sharp, if she'd never seen an elf. And she was unearthly, her beauty dreamlike, even in pain. Molly categorized this as well; she hadn't seen any sign of ache from any other elf in all her time with them. With the exception of torture, she amended, but she didn't like to think of those incidents. And then there was the look the woman's watcher wore. Though it was much like torture.

Her gaze automatically flicked to him, and her chest clenched as she realized he was staring at her now, not the woman. Not Cheerful, indeed. Molly immediately bowed her head, eyes on her lap as her fingers curled tightly into the blanket beneath her. *Not today*, she thought, *don't kill me today*.

21

Asher would come for her.

For his child.

He had to.

The dark-haired woman slept fitfully that night, but Molly did not think of her. She gave the fire her back and stared into the trees, watching the flames throw shadows like demons. She would live. Her son would live.

By dawn, Molly had slept little. The others were awake, nearly always awake, waiting for the woman. Molly didn't miss that the massive elf and the wiry elf had positioned themselves near her, and seemed to remain so afterward.

They rode further, the portentous darkness of the mountain a constant backdrop. She was never allowed to be alone, but the redhead did escort her from the group each day for some privacy.

It was on one of these occasions she knew for certain.

The redhead stayed near her, and though she gave Molly a few lengths' retreat, there was no question Molly would be caught if she intended escape. Molly's skirts were gathered as she walked through tangled brush. The redhead became slightly distracted, staring into a copse. Molly might have been more interested in what she saw next if they hadn't made her wait so long for this break. The redhead deftly scaled one of the trees, disappearing into the foliage.

Molly had known the elves were fast, nimble… not human, but she was always surprised to see it demonstrated. She shook her head as she raised her skirts higher and lowered herself behind the brush. She heard voices and froze, afraid of someone walking up on her.

But they hadn't known she was there.

"The human is dead weight." It was a deep voice, strong and low.

"It won't matter once she's back, none of this will matter."

Molly couldn't be sure who was speaking. Massive and Wiry? It couldn't be Cheerful, he'd never spoken with such loathing.

"He gives her too much. She does not have the capacity for this decision now."

There was a muffled thump, almost imperceptible, but it caused their conversation to halt.

Silence.

Molly nearly raised up then, but she heard one more comment. "It is right. You know that well."

She heard the clink of metal and stood, hastily straightening her skirts, to find the redhead walking in her direction. Behind her were the shadows of three large figures moving toward the horses. Molly looked up, speculating whether she was crazy for thinking the redhead had dropped from the trees into their conversation.

Their conversation about dead weight.

"Come."

The redhead gestured and Molly nodded, her mouth dry. She swallowed hard and stepped through the brush. Asher would come for her. For his child. He would.

They rode on. When they stopped for the day, she numbly took a seat on her blanket.

Some time passed before Cheerful spoke. "You are quiet this evening."

He made a comment about her wicked pup and grinned. She tried a smile but faltered. She felt a little ill.

"Are you well?" Cheerful asked, reaching up to lightly stroke her cheek, checking for heat.

In spite of it all, there was heat; a flush tore through her at his touch. He grinned wickedly at her response.

Suddenly, she lost all sense of balance. Her eyes floated for a moment before coming back to Steed. She swayed. *Wait, who's Steed?* Her eyes closed tight against the dizziness. And then she blacked out.

When Molly woke, they surrounded her. They helped her up to sitting, seeming to care whether she was sound. It would have made her feel better, except they seemed exceedingly concerned with her condition. Unnaturally so. But Molly didn't know what to do with that. She didn't know what to do with any of it.

Something was wrong.

The feeling stuck with her. They left her be for some time and then, later, Cheerful returned to his place beside her. He'd been toying with the pup, but without warning came nearer.

His proximity brought Molly from her daze, his tone this new, odd distress. "Feeling well, sunshine?"

Her mouth was dry. She licked her lips while searching for words.

"Something to drink, then?"

Unintentionally, Molly's eyes found the dark-haired woman's across the camp, met those dark emeralds and caught in their violent depths. Cheerful murmured something as he leaned forward to reach for the canteen on the blanket behind her.

Molly knew it wasn't an advance. But, for some reason, her arm swung full force as she slapped him across the face. It was only an instant, a flash of anger, before she was reeling.

Her vision fluttered and she squeezed her eyes shut, determined to control it. When she was certain she'd regained herself, she opened them again. She found him. Staring at her. She didn't think she was going to be calling him Cheerful any longer. He didn't *look* like he was going to kill her. *Not that they ever do*, she reminded herself.

She quickly opened her mouth to apologize, and then saw the puffy red welt and the offending hand flew up to cover her mouth. Had she hit him that hard? Molly was no maid, she had slapped men before, but playfully. She had never struck with such force; her hand had never followed through as boys did when they came to blows. Her palm still tingled from the contact, stung even.

"Are you well?" her victim asked in a level tone.

Her hand fell from her mouth but she was yet unable to find words. He waited, staring into her eyes as if examining her.

Once, Molly had slipped from her room to walk in the moonlight after a fine spring storm and found a field of freshly turned soil, dark with damp. She thought his eyes were richer than that brown; she thought she might get lost in them. They narrowed on her.

She cleared her throat. "Yes," she croaked. "Yes, I think I am well." She tried to appear remorseful.

He nodded, and then stood to join Wiry.

Molly was quiet after that. They all were. They rode several more days and she silently prayed for Asher. *Come for me*, she thought, *come for me now. Something is wrong.*

She had been sick twice. The first day, without inquiry, the redhead had offered her a preparation, but Molly only slid the powder into her pocket. She was wearing down, though, and when they passed a pond late one afternoon, Molly's stomach revolted against the scents.

The redhead appeared to notice her discomfort and gestured to Wiry, who suggested they stop for camp. Cheerful helped her from her horse and she leaned heavily on him for a moment, breathing deep against his chest. He felt sorry for her, she thought, for no real reason. And then she steadied herself and nodded, determined to overcome it.

But her resolve could only get her so far. It wasn't long after that she was on hands and knees in the cool grass as the redhead stood over her, watching her retch. She must have seen it coming, for she had practically dragged Molly from the camp only shortly before the convulsive heaving started.

After some time, there was nothing left. Molly cautiously raised to her knees, wiping her mouth with the back of her trembling hand. The redhead waited as Molly ran her fingers through her hair and smoothed her bodice, and then helped her to her feet, not releasing her arm until she was certain Molly could stand.

Molly took a deep breath and nodded, shaking her skirts out but not daring to bend over to straighten them properly. The redhead offered her a tonic but she waved it away, taking another breath as she indicated she was ready.

The redhead looked skeptical. But before she had a chance to say anything, her head cocked a fraction and she went still.

The action reminded Molly oddly of a dog. And then the red-head's posture changed suddenly, and it only added to the effect.

It caused Molly to recall her pup and she glanced down to find him at her skirts, sniffing what she sincerely hoped was only earth smeared across the hem.

She didn't feel like carrying him, but the redhead had scooped him up, pushed him into the pouch, and slung it over Molly's shoulder before she had any opportunity to protest. Shortly, she was being pressed out of the trees and into the clearing where they had camped.

Molly knew something was wrong instantly. The clearing was silent as Cheerful and Wiry stood near the center, backs to her. They were in front of the dark-haired woman, protecting her. The woman stared on between them and Molly's gaze followed.

Her heart skipped as she saw a cloaked figure in the distance with Not Cheerful. *Asher*, she thought, *come for me*. Her knees gave a fraction but she caught herself. The redhead didn't seem to notice, only holding her firm grip on Molly's arm.

And then the cloaked figure turned and Molly could see golden curls from under the hood. It was a woman. Not Asher.

She felt sick. Her hand automatically fell to her stomach. He had not come for her, for his child.

The newcomer's head flicked toward Molly then, her eyes hard. The dark-haired woman turned to see what had the new-comer's attention, confusion in her gaze. And then there was a low voice—a muttered curse, Molly thought—before the dark-haired woman's eyes lost focus and rolled back into her head.

Molly watched as the woman collapsed into the arms of her protectors, only half aware as the cloaked figure appeared before her, speaking two more words that sent Molly into blackness.

She was confident she'd been out for days when she finally came to. Her limbs were weak, her mouth parched, her stomach hollow… Molly jerked upright despite the fatigue, her hand finding her stomach.

"There, there," a soothing voice purred from beside her. She jumped and cursed, curving her arm around her middle. "No harm will come to you, child," the woman assured her.

Molly stared, working to clear the muddle of her mind. The woman waited patiently as Molly took in her surroundings, the small room with makeshift cot, blankets, supplies, food, all doing their part to calm her. She took a deep breath and continued to scan, her eyes finally focusing on the woman, falling over her light cloth pants, her deep brown shirt, narrowing on the golden wisps that fell around her face.

"What did you do to me?" Molly seethed when she recognized the woman as the cloaked figure from the camp.

"I have not harmed you," the woman replied coolly.

Molly's eyebrows rose.

The woman remained composed, merely shaking her head, and Molly took stock. She guessed she wasn't hurt, only ill as she had been before the incident. But she was outraged. Her mouth opened to hurl accusations at her captor, but before she could speak, a sharp pain sliced through her side.

She cried out, clutching the source. The woman reached toward her and Molly wrenched away.

"It is not I who cause you this pain," she said, indicating Molly's stomach.

Molly could not respond, only breathe through clenched teeth as she waited for it to pass. When the woman tried again, Molly didn't fight her.

"How long?" she asked as she slid a warm hand against the curve of Molly's waist.

Molly didn't answer.

"You are only hurting yourself, child." She pressed two fingers below Molly's ribs and the pain dulled and then subsided.

Molly's panting quieted and she lay back against the pillows. She would not trust this woman.

She lay still, settling her breathing, and all the while the woman sat wordlessly beside her.

"Why did you take me?" Molly eventually asked.

"Many reasons, child."

Molly sat up, angry again. "Stop calling me child."

The woman looked doubtful. There was a slight twist to the corner of her mouth but Molly couldn't tell if she was mocking her. She had a gorgeous smirk, if that was what it was. Her lips were the same flushed pink as her cheeks and her eyes sparkled. Like shattered glass in the sun. Like light catching ripples in water...

Molly shook herself, unsettled.

The woman smiled then and the change in her face took Molly's breath. She was a vision, ethereal and strong.

"Who are you?" Molly whispered.

"Juniper Fountain, daughter of Elerias."

"Are you"—Molly swallowed—"a fairy?"

Juniper snorted.

Molly was suddenly embarrassed. "You're just how they described them is all. And you're so different than the others. And, well, I've never met one, so how would I know?"

Juniper's smile faded. "Yes." She was silent for a moment, and then recalled herself. At the woman's mild smile, Molly had the errant thought that she needed something from her. "Ahh, but dear, I saw you with the fire fairy."

Molly stared at her blankly. A fire fairy? She recalled the illustrations from her books, remembered the descriptions of the wicked red ones, the flicker of the flames.

The redhead. How could Molly have been so oblivious?

"Curses," she snapped, startling the woman as she smacked her palm to her face in disbelief. All her life she'd wanted to meet a fairy. This one had watched her pee.

Molly realized she'd gotten sidetracked. "So, you're an elf?"

Juniper nodded. "I am of the light elves."

"And the others?" Molly asked timidly.

"Dark, of the North." She could see the question in Molly's eyes. "You should be glad I have taken you. They would have disposed of you."

Molly nodded. She'd expected as much. But now she was further from Asher, for he was Lord of the North. "And what will you do with me?" she asked.

"Help you," Juniper answered.

The days turned to weeks and Juniper did help her. But there was only so much that could be done, and Molly's condition deteriorated quickly. Molly had seen women ill while carrying before. She had helped with some of the villagers when needed. She knew this was not such an illness. This was something else. Something was wrong.

She had been suffering from tremors, plagued with strange sensations, once as if she were floating, occasionally as if she were afire. Juniper had eased the pains for the most part, but these odd impressions were unsettling. And they were getting worse.

Juniper had stopped leaving her alone, though. At first, she'd depart for one or two days, leaving Molly with supplies and powders, tonics and instructions. It had taken Molly a few weeks to realize the trips would come after questions of her travels, details of her captors, particulars of surroundings she'd remembered.

But she hadn't gone lately. Molly couldn't be sure whether it was because of Molly's state, or because Juniper had accepted that Molly had no idea where to find Asher. It couldn't be called trust, the bond she had developed with Juniper, but she had no other option but to rely on the woman. Molly knew there was more, so much that she did not understand, but she had to stay alive for Asher. For her son.

"Drink," Juniper insisted. "The fevers are burning your fluids off."

"I'm not being stubborn," Molly maintained, "you know I can't keep it down."

"Drink," she repeated.

Molly scowled and Juniper laughed, a sound that had been noticeably absent of late.

"What's so funny?" Molly asked, piqued.

"Nothing, child. You simply remind me of someone."

"Who?"

"Only someone I used to care for. Someone of your age."

A shadow passed over Juniper's face and Molly asked, "Where is she now?"

Something similar to a hum escaped as Juniper considered her answer. "She is in between."

Molly assumed that must have been an elf term.

"Ah, Freya," Juniper mumbled as she refilled her own glass.

Molly froze. The action caught Juniper's eye and her gaze narrowed on Molly.

"I know of her," Molly whispered. The words came of their own accord. "She is *his.*"

Juniper's jaw went tight, her eyes to ice. "You know nothing."

Molly jerked up, ready to fight, but the action caused a tremor.

It was a bad one. Her throat constricted for a moment, and then her skin began to burn.

Juniper grabbed her arms. "Calm yourself. Breathe. Remain still."

Molly felt her head shaking. *No, no, no.* This was wrong. It shouldn't be like this. Something was wrong. Fire and razors tore through her midsection, her hands went numb. Panic-stricken, she looked to Juniper.

"I cannot help you, child. There is nothing to be done." Every word was sincere.

Molly only had one question, and it was clear.

"The child will live," Juniper answered.

But you will not.

Pain ripped through Molly, her body convulsed, and then she was granted one moment of reprieve to gasp for air. She was suddenly soaked with sweat, shuddering violently before the cold turned back to fire. Every inch of skin was ablaze, every hair a needle, every breath an ache so severe to not breathe would have been relief. But she could not give.

She forced each breath, thankful for the pain. The pain meant she had not surrendered.

Her chest rose from the cot in a spasm and then she fell back, grinding and twisting uncontrollably against the torture. Tears flowed from her eyes and her mouth tasted of copper. Her fingers clutched at the blanket beneath her, searching for purchase, something to pull herself up.

Juniper pressed her back. "Be still, child, be still," she murmured.

Molly convulsed again, gagged, and then bore down as the knife pain cut through her once more.

He's not coming, she thought. *He's not coming and it will be too late.*

Her hands found her midsection and she pulled air through her nose, biting down on the agony to force words through clenched teeth. "You have to find him."

Juniper brushed the damp strands of hair off Molly's face without responding.

"You have to find him," Molly repeated. "Take my son to him."

Juniper did not answer, but Molly could see her doubt through the haze of tears.

"He will not come in time," Molly explained. "I am his favorite. His chosen. My son will be king."

Juniper stared down at the girl who was dying to bring Asher a child. *His favorite.* How long had this been going on? How many more were there?

The girl bucked convulsively against the magic rending her from within, and Junnie sighed, readying herself for what was to come. Not simply the next hours in this camp, but the deadly months ahead for everyone.

Mother save you, Freya, she thought, *there will be an army of them.*

RISE *of the*
SEVEN

1

FREY

I couldn't say I wasn't disappointed when I got my memory back. Somehow, I'd expected to be smoother. I'd thought the old me was exceptionally clever, sharp, sure-footed. She had been in line for the throne, after all. I'd nearly convinced myself the ineptness was all because of the bonds, because they'd messed with my brain. But it wasn't. And not only had I retained a good deal of awkwardness, it seemed worse, because everyone was watching me now.

I held back a sigh as my gaze again traveled the room full of elves, all eyes on me. Their Lord of the North. I straightened my shoulders, which were heavy with thick armored plates, my new decoration for formal gatherings. A lean, raven-haired elf who I recognized as once being a leader in the eastern range seemed to make the decision to approach but, before he'd moved more than three steps, Rider was in front of him, matching his height. I glanced at Rhys, who appeared to be scanning the room for others who would attempt approach, and decided I'd had enough. I stood, hand sliding to rest on the hilt of the sword at my waist as I addressed the crowd.

"Your attendance is greatly appreciated. Please enjoy the feast and the wine. Good evening."

As I stepped down, the room was silent. I could see the smirk on Anvil's broad face but didn't care. I turned from the gathering and slipped out of the room. I knew I needed to keep up appearances, but I really hated castle politics. My guard had been doing what they could, keeping the most troublesome leaders from a private conference. And they had handled the stream of subjects who'd lined up at the season change for audience with me. *Me, Lord of the North.*

I snorted, shaking my head, and someone laughed. I looked up to find Grey, leaning against a corridor wall, watching me. His smile held a thousand secrets. "What?" I demanded, defensive.

He simply smiled, pushing off the wall to join me. "And where are we headed?"

I didn't have the slightest idea. "The library."

He laughed again, seeing through the fib with ease. "To see Ruby, I presume?"

Agh, I hadn't known she was there. Ruby, though I considered her invaluable in my guard, still felt the need to hide because before I'd been bound, northern rule hadn't exactly tolerated fairies. It was something I'd have to work on changing.

"I'd like to see if she's made any progress," I lied. The moment I saw her she'd spill whatever she'd been researching, so it was a safe lie.

Grey only smiled. His devotion to Ruby was boundless, but he knew her character as well as I did and better. She was going to be in a state.

Her head popped up the moment we entered the room, red curls bouncing with the movement. "Well, that was fast," she chided. She glanced out the window as if she were checking the height of the sun, though it was dark with night. "You'll not establish yourself as Lord of the North by running out on guests after a matter of minutes."

We all knew I'd made it at least an hour, but I didn't argue the point. "I mean to make a reputation as a mysterious captain."

"Mysterious and all-powerful," she replied, then changed the subject as my jaw tightened. It was no secret I was uncomfortable with my new strength. It would have been enough to have regained my own power, but I'd been inundated with that of Asher and all those before him. I could still see his lips move, a silent stream of the words that would release me, the recital that would drive the forces of so many he had taken into my very soul.

"So, I found several stories regarding the wolves," she announced, pulling me from my trance.

I smiled. She'd been obsessed with Finn and Keaton since the moment she'd found I'd known them before, and I'd not been willing to give up their secrets. Truth be told, I didn't entirely know the whole story, but it was fun to mess with Ruby.

She grimaced. It annoyed the fire out of her. Occasionally, I felt a little guilty about it because, after all, she had helped deliver me from the evils of Grand Council, but it was too entertaining not to keep up and it wasn't like she didn't have it coming after what she'd put me through when I was bound.

She snapped the book she'd been reading shut. My cheeks tightened, fighting to pull back the smile, and her expression nearly caused laughter to boil up.

Grey intervened. "Well, since Freya has left us without the benefit of the feast, I say we head to the kitchen."

Ruby took a deep breath, leveled her shoulders, and walked right past us.

"I think she preferred the old me." I laughed as Grey and I followed.

Her head poked back through the door as we were nearly to it, and she started to speak, thought better of it, and turned to continue on her way. I saw Grey's smile out of the corner of my eye.

Ruby's posture changed the instant she stepped through the kitchen door. She exclaimed, "Steed!" and bounced forward to greet her brother.

I felt like the wind had been knocked out of me. I glanced nervously around the room. My eye caught Steed's and he grinned, sly and sexy. "He wasn't hungry."

I forced my expression into confusion, though I knew exactly who he meant. Every one of us did.

Steed stepped toward me. "You look well, sunshine."

I laughed. He'd been such a charmer when I was bound, but now his banter was only for play. There was someone else for me. My stomach turned, and I had to bite down before I asked where he was.

It had been an underhanded thing to do, I knew that. But as we'd stood among the remains of battle, after all was settled and my memories returned, I had panicked. I had been over-whelmed with the power I held, the emotions that threatened to run feral, the realization of all that had happened and what would follow. And I'd been a coward. Plain and simple.

I'd been aware of his eyes on me the entire time, and, as we finalized affairs, I'd ordered him and Steed away. I could still see the look on his face, the set of his jaw, the strain of muscle at his neck and shoulder. I'd directed them to finish off Asher's guard, his supporters. To find and eliminate them. *Make a show of it*, I'd said. *The kingdom will know I've returned.*

It was the last thing I'd said to him. I had been certain I would figure out what to do, how to deal with it, get a handle on my emotions. That had been nearly two weeks ago. My palms felt clammy but I couldn't decide whether the anxiousness was because I wanted, *needed* to see him, or because I was coward still.

"No," Ruby said, "I didn't like the old you better."

My gaze snapped to her.

"You were fun, yes, but you got that vacant stare." She narrowed her eyes on me. "And I could never tell where you were." Ruby smiled, making it clear she knew exactly where my mind was now.

I brushed past her to where Grey and Steed leaned against the table. They'd apparently been watching my daze as well. Grey offered me something to eat but I had absolutely no interest.

I needed to get out of there, badly.

"I'm glad you're back," I said as I turned to Steed.

He looked doubtful, but he gave me a smile anyway. "I am, too. Can't wait to see what you've done with the place."

I nodded and excused myself.

When I hit the hall, I had to force myself to remain standing, not to bend over, brace myself on my knees, and hyperventilate. I had myself under control, the fear back in check. I was ashamed of it, and I'd been determined to overcome it. I'd just not been able to do that yet. And the realization scared me even worse.

It felt out of control, the wave of need that accompanied any thought of him. And I had a lot of thoughts about him. A lot. Most of them centered around the one night I'd spent in his arms. But that wasn't what scared me—that had been incredible. What scared me was what that night stood for, what I had, or had nearly, sacrificed for it. I had—no, we *all* had—gone through so much to restore myself from the bonds forced upon me by Council, only to fall into a new set, just as dangerous.

The problem was, I couldn't decide whether these bonds had taken. I felt the need, yes. I felt the yearning, the pull. I knew the connection was in place, but I couldn't know if it was a full bond. It didn't feel secure enough, not as I'd been warned it would happen. I couldn't be sure whether that was due to the fact that I'd been bound already, my magic not fully in place, or because I was not wholly elf. Because I was half human. There was no way to know how that type of bond would affect me. But when his eyes were on me, I would run right back into his arms. If the bond wasn't set already, it would be the instant I got close enough to touch him.

It was why I'd sent him away, though I could never admit it. There was too much at stake.

I reached out and traced the cool stone of the wall as I walked. It had long been a habit of mine, reminding me of my childhood years, running carefree through these corridors, arms out-stretched as if in flight. My laughter had echoed through the halls, whether alone or being chased by Chevelle. The touch centered me now. My fingers trailed lazily around the corner as I walked through the door to my room.

And froze as I found Chevelle.

2

CHEVELLE

Chevelle leaned casually back in the chair, though the set of his mouth proved he was anything but. He still wore his traveling clothes, dark leather and an assortment of blades. I forced myself to move, walking my fingers the last few inches of door frame before lowering them to my side in artificial nonchalance.

He didn't speak.

I felt the hand I'd lowered slide up my leg and, before I had a chance to fiddle nervously with it, raised it to tuck the hair behind my ear. The gesture seemed to unnerve him, and that made me want to smile.

I watched him watch me for a moment. But it wasn't going anywhere good. *Right, then.*

"Were you able to locate the remainder of the guard?" I asked, forcing any emotion from my tone.

"Mostly. Axe, Frost, Steele, and Waters proved difficult. It appears they were warned."

"Anyone of note unfound?"

"Only Rowan, but he has a knack for such."

I nodded. Knowing Rowan, he might not resurface for a century. He was one of Asher's best guards, and his talent for stealth was legendary. "And you made a show of them?"

"Oh, yes," he answered grimly. "We made quite a spectacle of it."

"News has not traveled back to us. Have you received any word of reaction?"

He really didn't want to answer.

I waited.

"Not all were convinced. I would suggest a gathering."

It was not what I wanted to hear, and Chevelle saw my hesitation. I'd developed some bad habits during the time I'd spent bound. I'd been working to regain the control I'd spent my childhood forming, the ability to mask emotion that seemed to come so easily to the others. I nearly had it mastered, but Chevelle knew me well.

"This isn't simply your distaste for exhibition."

"No," I answered.

His patience astounded me. I glanced down at my hands, and then faced him, chin up. "I am having some trouble controlling the magic."

He stood and crossed to me, the slightest hint of worry in his gaze. "The bindings?"

"No, no," I assured him. "Not my magic. His." The magic Asher had given me.

"Should we try to undo the casting?"

"No!" It might have been overemphatic, but I hated spells. There was no way to be sure of Asher's methods and so much could go wrong. It wasn't worth it.

"Then there is nothing left but to practice."

I bit my cheek to keep from commenting.

Silence hung between us for a moment and then in a soft voice, he asked, "Are you well, Freya?"

My heart clenched. I could only nod.

"I know this is far from over," he said, "but I feel you are safer now than in the village."

I knew it wasn't his fault, knew what had happened was beyond all of our control. And I could see his guilt, just as I felt my own, but none of us were entirely blameless either.

It must have been hard for everyone, but I had been bound, unaware during so much of it. I shook off a chill. I'd been imprisoned in the village by an unwilling Council.

"It was a long time." I let it sit there, not exactly an accusation, but close enough.

"Yes, it was," Chevelle answered, and it tasted of regret.

But there was nothing to do now but move on.

"A banquet, then," I supplied.

He nodded. "I will arrange it."

"And practice." I grimaced, for old times' sake.

He smiled genuinely then, and I ached at the contrast with the pain he'd worn only moments ago. He started to reach for me and then caught himself, and the gesture made me want his touch so badly that I wondered if I *had* been truly bound to him.

That was the only thing that kept me from closing the distance between us.

"You should rest," he said. "I will meet you for practice in the morning. Our usual time?"

I laughed. It hadn't been usual for a long time. And there hadn't been much practice involved.

He moved a breath closer and whispered, "Sleep well, Freya," before walking past me out the door.

I had to pinch myself to keep from following him.

I loosed the straps on my armor and shrugged it off, tossing it on the table by the door. That was when I saw the box.

It sat centered on the narrow wooden table, alone. I wasn't sure how long I watched it before I moved, but when I finally reached for it, my hands shook. I had to sit down. Laying the box on the bed, I curled my legs up in front of it, terrified of opening it.

Asher had taken everything from me. My mother, my freedom, my safety. But, given the enormity of those things, it was often the small treasures that I'd thought of most. They were naught but tiny remembrances that had given me comfort. In his attempt to control me, he had taken even those.

Those last bloody days had been the tipping point for my mother, I was certain. Had I known the outcome, I might have let the tokens go, might have yielded to Asher. They meant little compared to her life. But I had fought him harder then, as if that infraction was the worst of it, when he had done so much more. I had not the temperament of the others. The elves were stoic, but when pushed too far chanced being overcome, unable to return to themselves. I had to fight to hide my emotion, but it could come and go as the winds, leaving me no worse for the storm.

There was no wind now as I opened the carved stone lid. On top was a letter, a small note folded in half. I laid it aside and pulled a strip of silk from the box. My fingers ran across the soft fabric, a piece of my mother's favorite dress. When Asher had confined her, these scraps had accompanied her messages, so I would know them truly hers. I held it to my nose, breathed in the scent of her. She was rain and honeysuckle, a cool winter night. Her scent was a contradiction, as was she. She was of light and dark. And I of both and my father. I had often wondered what that made me. When we were young, I had asked Chevelle what I smelled like. Without hesitation, he'd answered, "Wet elk."

With a smile, I returned the scrap to the box and touched the smooth stones, gold ring, and leather strap that lay inside. The amulet was there. I wondered if Chevelle had known its origin. The inky blue had reminded me so much of its owner, Sapphire.

We both blamed Asher for her death. Though I shared that blame with myself. I had been a fool to think we could escape him. After all he had done, I had known there was no true escape. Somewhere, deep down, I had to have understood what I was risking. There was no doubt that such blatant defiance would have to be answered. And I had not cared about the cost. Until we'd found her.

I could still see her lifeless body cradled in Chevelle's arms. I could feel the anger, taste the bile, recall the first flavor of hatred. Nothing else could have driven me to seek such a final revenge. She had been an innocent. They had cleaved her eyes from their sockets because I'd intended to walk away from all of it, to leave with him. They had never acknowledged her in life, but here they had dressed her in a royal gown, adorned her with jewels.

His mother. The blue of her eyes a message to me. The same depthless sapphire as Chevelle's.

Chevelle had returned these items to me. Though they meant little now, they had once been precious. I'd no doubt they had been a trial to recover. I didn't know if I had the courage to read his note, but my hand moved numbly toward it.

I took a deep breath and opened the fold. Two small words, but they changed everything.

My love.

Chevelle knew me. He'd given me all that he could and left me to decide.

My head fell and I put the note in the box, closed the lid, and slid it into the hiding spot beneath the third stone under the floor of my bed. I walked out of the room without looking back, turned down the corridor, and ran.

Six doors, two stairways, and one window later, I was scaling the last ten feet to a roof of the castle. I'd stolen a cloak on my way and when I reached the top, the wind caught and flipped it behind me with a snap. My hair whipped my face as I made my way across to perch on the only point that was blocked from wind by the tower but still allowed a full view of the mountain below and sky ahead. I wrapped the cloak tightly around me and felt settled for the first time in days.

It was silent for two hours, and then the quick, light padding of paws approached. Keaton and Finn.

They settled in beside me. Their silvery fur caught the moonlight in an ethereal glow.

"I can't leave him," I said.

The wolves did not respond.

"I may not be able to be with him, but I cannot leave."

3

MEETING

I woke on the perch as the sun broke the clouds. My first thoughts were curses; I should have met Chevelle at dawn. I hurried down, running until I reached the corridor and saw the servants. I didn't recognize them, but that was no surprise, considering so many of them had had to be removed after they'd been found out as Asher's spies. The castle was fully staffed now and each of them, uniformed and mannered, prepared for the banquet. Chevelle had been busy. Remembering my own station, I straightened my shoulders and slowed my pace.

When I reached the practice room, I thought he'd given up on me. I walked into the empty space for the first time since I'd regained myself fully. It held an echo of memory, emotion. I walked further, glancing up to see the morning sun stream in the filigreed windows, catching dust motes in its rays. I sighed, thinking of how it must have looked to him when I hadn't shown up after the gift he'd left me. And then I saw him.

He stepped forward. He'd been on the ledge, probably watching out a window while he waited. He stopped, the sun

49

at his back throwing his features into further shade, and I had a flash of nervousness. I didn't know if I could pull this off.

I straightened. "I fell asleep."

I thought I saw the corner of his mouth pull up, but couldn't be positive. He jumped down and crossed to me.

"Good," he said, "you'll need your rest."

Sleep had once been a sore subject with me. I'd required about twice as much as the others and I used to fight it, trying to keep up with them. Chevelle knew that. He'd seen what I'd done to myself.

I'd been different in so many ways, and he knew them all. Things didn't work the same with me. I wasn't born with the natural instinct for magic. I'd always had to work at it, find the power and force the control. But I had overcome it. And now I had a new problem.

"So," I started, "practice."

"Show me what you've got," he answered.

I really didn't want to do this, but I closed my eyes, centered my breathing, and released. The stones beneath our feet started to vibrate and shift, the walls shook, the iron in the window let loose an ear-piercing metallic creak. Tiny sprinkles of rock fell onto my face and I stopped, sealing the stones back in place before opening my eyes once more.

He looked dubious.

"Yep," I said. "And that's not even angry."

"You've been angry?" he asked.

"Ruby's been here."

It was clearly a joke, but he didn't laugh. Not even a little. And then I smiled as I realized how much he'd been forced to deal with her antics while I'd been bound. I wondered what she'd put him through.

"You chose her," I reminded him.

"I used to think so," he said.

I chuckled. "Things do tend to have a way of working out for her."

"Cursed fairies," he grumbled.

"Cursed fairies," I agreed.

"Do you have a plan for tomorrow's demonstration?" he asked, clearly determined to change the subject.

"I think I'll wing it."

"Brilliant."

We were silent for a moment. Finally, he asked, "Fire?"

"All right," I answered with little confidence.

He stepped beside me so we were both facing the long, empty space and used his magic to chuck a rock from the box in the corner. As it flew across the room, I raised my arm and pointed at it in an attempt to focus solely on striking it with a fireball. Not one flame lit but the rock exploded.

"What was that?" Chevelle asked.

I shrugged. "Did I mention sometimes it doesn't work properly?"

He nodded, expressionless. "This time, try to shatter the stone."

Another rock launched from the box, flying straight into the expanse. I focused on splitting it and it burst into dust. I looked to Chevelle.

He tore a small piece of fabric from the hem of his shirt and held it before me. "Burn this." I started to glance down, but the first finger of his other hand stopped me. "Not my palm."

Right.

I concentrated on the fabric for a moment before the idea of burning his palm recalled one of those odd, not-quite-me memories. The lines of a map burnt into my palms. An old trick we'd used on Fannie. It was only a fraction of a second before I realized I'd gotten angry.

I gasped at Chevelle's intake of breath and raised my hands in a helpless gesture as the flames died down.

"I see what you mean," Chevelle said through clenched teeth.

"Ah, I'm sorry. I just... I got irritated for a second. Let's just call it even."

"Aye."

"And," I continued, "in case you've forgotten, we are in agreement that you'll not use spells near me unless absolutely necessary."

He stared me straight in the eye. "We are even from here."

My jaw rolled involuntarily. Come to think of it, there'd been a lot of catching up on his end while I'd been bound. "Fine," I answered, taking a step toward him.

We stared at each other for one long moment and then the unburned hand clenched into a fist. When I'd been bound, I had thought him constantly angry with me. But I knew him again, and I understood this was a different kind of restraint. He wouldn't touch me, he'd let me decide.

When I didn't respond, he stepped back. "The others will be waiting."

With a promise to continue practice in the morning, we made our way to Anvil's study. Asher had always met with his guard in the throne room, keeping it a formal matter, but I didn't care for the echo of the high ceilings or sitting elevated among those who protected me. And it wasn't as if Anvil ever used his library.

It was a small room compared to the other meeting places in the castle. A long oval table was centered at one end, a few plush chairs sat at the other. High windows cast odd shadows in the corners, but the natural light focused on the flat of the table. Scattered about the room were my guard.

They came together, each taking their place around the oval, Chevelle at my right. It was then, as I stood before them, that I realized this was my first meeting of the guard as Elfreda, Lord of the North. I resisted the urge to run a hand over my face. This was something I had never wanted. I forced myself to stand tall and meet the eyes of each of the seven before me. The seven who would enforce my rule, the seven who would give their lives to defend me.

I spoke their names as my gaze connected with each, a tradition that outdated this castle. "Chevelle Vattier." He was no stranger to the formalities and he stood at his post with confidence. I could almost see the promise in his eyes.

Grey waited to Chevelle's right. He was quick and loyal, and I was lucky to have him. "Grey of Camber." He gave a small nod in answer.

My eyes followed to Rhys and Rider. I knew little of the brothers, but I trusted Finn and Keaton, and as I spoke their names they pledged themselves as well.

"Steed Summit." Steed had gotten involved by chance, or so Ruby would have us believe. But he had proven himself.

"Ruby Summit." I nearly smiled at the heat radiating from her. I would never know if it was pride at her new station or the idea of all the trouble she could get into here. But it didn't matter. Not after what we'd been through.

"Reed of Keithar Peak." Anvil inclined his head, shoulders straight. He, like Chevelle, understood his place at this table and held above all else his duty.

I took a slow, steadying breath and then began as if this were not a monstrous undertaking. "Chevelle tells me he and Steed were successful. However, it seems we have some convincing left to do." Only two of my guard were familiar with castle politics. I had a feeling Ruby would fit right in, but she presented a whole new problem. We were going to have to play this out as Asher would have, and that left a bitter taste in my mouth. "Chevelle has suggested a banquet." Anvil nodded. The rest of the table sat silent. "A show of power," I explained.

I deferred to Chevelle, who outlined the details and responsibilities of each of them. Who should watch which clan leader, who should cover which areas, which signals meant what or whom. Everyone had a task, everyone had their role. Except Ruby.

When Chevelle finished, he glanced at me, a question in his eyes. I nodded grimly, giving him permission.

"Frey has an issue with control." A snigger escaped from Ruby's side of the table but my glare cut it short. Chevelle continued. "We will meet each morning to assist in her recovery."

"Why do we not simply cast—" Anvil's words were cut short as an intensified version of the glare narrowed on him.

"Again," I stated as clear and loud as possible, "there will be no use of spells on or near me without absolute necessity."

Steed raised his hand. It wouldn't have been funny if I hadn't spent time in the village and seen the schoolchildren, but I had, and it was a struggle not to laugh. Ruby smacked him.

"If you are planning to inquire as to why, don't," I warned.

So far, this was nothing like Asher's meeting of the guards.

I moved on. "The banquet is settled. Is there any news to table?"

Grey spoke up. "There is word of the new Council. Whispers of Juniper's plans have flooded Camber."

"We have heard such as well," Rider put in. "It is said she has gathered a following, not only among the villagers, but some of the rogue southern clans."

"There is no evidence," I said.

"You've seen her cloak," Anvil offered in a decidedly non-confrontational tone.

"She is no longer of Grand Council, what else would she wear?"

They were silent for a moment. I couldn't help but defend her. Junnie was all the family I had left. She'd given up leadership in Grand Council to protect me, stayed near me in the village. Sure, she had disagreed with what they were doing. They had killed my mother when by right she was owed their protection. Junnie had taken umbrage with their attack on the North, she had suspicions about their plans, but she'd given up everything. Besides, the villages and forests were none of my business. I wasn't Asher.

I dismissed the subject and the meeting, with a reminder of practice at dawn. As the others left the room, Ruby stopped to examine a book on the wall shelves. I sat at the head of the table, thinking of all to come. My demonstration at the banquet would have to be severe. Not only did my mere existence as a half-human cause issue, but now rumors of a new Council were running rampant. A stronger Council to replace that which had nearly destroyed the North. Even I had seen Junnie's sigil. I could not deny the possibility. I would have to assert my rule without doubt tomorrow.

I felt the corner of my mouth pull up.

"Ruby," I asked, "how would you like to start some trouble?"

4

PRACTICE

We met in the largest practice room. The sight of the others there reminded me so much of the group practice session when I'd been bound, I had to laugh. I had been so certain then that one wrong move could have destroyed me. But Chevelle had chosen these men. I understood now that he'd trusted them all with my life. He'd had to, when an errant thought or moment of temper could cost you your sparring partner. I knew they could not hurt me now, but I had not realized then that their magic would never have touched me in more than the annoyingly painful way they had used it to teach me.

I tried to keep in mind they'd been doing it to protect me.

"Me first," came from Ruby right away. Apparently, my promise of trouble for this evening had not sated her.

I smiled. "Ready when you are."

A tingle ran up my back and I knew she'd attempted a sneak attack. I squelched her flame but raised my hands to the side and ran my own flame down my arms to light in my palms, as if I'd stolen hers. If she wanted to play dirty, I had my own tricks. The floor lit behind her as she readied her next attack. I flung my outstretched arms forward and released the fire. Ruby didn't even flinch. Until it turned to icy blue mist that showered against her.

She cursed and pulled the whip from her side. *Oh, yes*, I thought, *I do owe her*.

The tongue lit as it curled around and she began to shift her weight from foot to foot, priming herself for another attempt. She cracked the whip at the right side of my face, missing it by a hair's breadth, while simultaneously throwing a fireball at my left thigh from the side. A burst of white stopped the flame from touching me and another headed toward her stomach. She leapt quickly out of the way and then set the room ablaze.

Flames surrounded us, engulfing our section of the practice room. It was impressive.

I had planned to smother the fire, but something went wrong. The floor beneath Ruby fell. She caught herself and the conflagration died.

"Not okay, Frey," Ruby complained.

I stepped forward to help her. "It wasn't my intention."

When she was on her feet, we stared into the hole in the floor.

"Where are the stones?" Ruby asked.

I shrugged.

"Are you sure this is safe?" Grey asked from beside her.

I looked up, catching the concern in Chevelle's eyes. "Maybe I'll just practice on my own from now on," I suggested.

Rhys put in, "I believe it will be safest if we assist you."

All eyes fell on the two tall, slender elves.

Rider explained. "Though we are not twins, we are brothers and share a connection. We have the ability to combine our powers."

Stunned silence followed. Finally, Steed spoke up. "How does that work?"

"Usually, only one of us has control. Clearly, we cannot both command it. We essentially borrow the other's energy while directing our own," Rhys explained.

A quick glance at Chevelle confirmed he had not been aware of their rare talent. Certainly the wolves had been.

"Is it possible then," Grey asked, "that the same technique could be used to direct Frey's power?"

"You mean to displace it?" Ruby asked.

"No, I was thinking of it not being entirely of her and therefore Asher's power could possibly be split from her own. But displacement may be a better option."

"Would I be able to do that?" I asked Rider. "Can you send one another your power, or would I have to allow someone to borrow from me?"

"It is impossible to guess." Rider contemplated the idea for a moment. "When we borrow, it is with a shared will. I am unsure whether it can be done otherwise, without that connection."

I thought again of the wolves. This was no coincidence.

Rhys spoke up. "There is a danger in trying without the connection." No one wanted to ask how he knew, but he could see our interest. "We discovered the link as children, quite by accident. I was under attack and would undoubtedly fall. My assailant was toying with me, enjoying the torment as he forced my brother to watch."

My stomach turned as his words recalled the memory of Chevelle's prone form writhing in agony.

"As I lay on the floor, listening to Rider's shouts of protest over the sound of my own horrified screams, all I could think was that if I were as strong as him, if I had his power, I would crush this black terror standing over me. And he could think of nothing but saving me, giving me his own life in order to keep me alive, to defeat the elves attacking us."

Anvil was generally not the meddlesome type, so his question surprised me. "Why were you attacked?"

Rider nodded. "It was some time before we understood that ourselves. At that point, we were very young, too inexperienced to grasp the extent of the situation. We were unaware that the entire kingdom was fearful of us. Some spoke of prophecy, others dared not speak of us at all. The pair of us were blamed for each calamity that came upon the realm, each misfortune of the king, though we were merely boys. The mob that came for us had no reason but fear and superstition. And possibly clandestine orders from their ruler."

I started to speak but faltered. Their tale was too reminiscent of raw memories.

Rhys finished out Rider's explanation. "The irony is their attack gave us the ability they feared. Forced it upon us. Our response to that action not only revealed to us our full strength, but turned it against them."

The room was silent for a long moment.

"The danger?" Chevelle finally asked.

"Yes," Rhys answered, coming back from what was plainly an emotional memory. "I doubt there would be issue with an attempt to borrow from Frey. But we have found it is impossible to give the power to others without injuring them."

"They take it as a strike," Rider explained. With a hint of chagrin, he added, "We also learned such by accident. As children."

"Didn't help our cause," Rhys said.

I had my doubts, but I was positive the wolves had not brought these men from the ice lands without good reason. "I will try." Several of the others immediately bristled at the idea, but before they had a chance to voice their arguments I held up a hand. "Not today. I have a few things to check on first."

"I will research the archives for the twins," Ruby said.

"Thank you," I replied, though I was fairly certain she'd have no luck there. When I had a free moment, I would have to find the wolves, and hope they would give me some indication if we were on the right track.

"I think we should break for now," I suggested. "I don't feel I can overcome this in one day and I'm confident you all have other tasks before this evening's event."

The group split into small sets, obviously agitated by the new plan. I glanced at Chevelle, unable to remove the painful image Rhys' story brought to mind. His eyes met mine and I could see that he understood. As he stood speaking with Anvil, his hand rose to his collar and he slid the material between his thumb and forefinger. I smiled and did the same. Funny how the small gesture meant more now, with Asher gone, than when we'd conceived it to subvert him.

Ruby grabbed my elbow and pulled me from the room, chattering about her ideas on the new theory. I let her.

When we reached the hall, Grey and Steed were standing together, deep in conversation. Ruby released her grip on me and immediately started a new discussion with Grey, drawing him down the hall with her.

Steed shrugged and laughed, apparently resigned to finishing his exchange with Grey later. "Hungry?" he asked.

"Ravenous." I smiled and walked with him toward the dining room.

When we were alone in the corridor, he slowed his pace. "I've been meaning to apologize."

I glanced at him curiously.

"If I had known… Frey, I never would have…"

"Oh." I stopped him when I realized he was referring to his interest in me. "No, I cannot blame you for that."

He smirked. I smacked his arm. "What I mean is, I can't charge you for what neither of us knew."

"Still," he said, "I do express my regret." And then he smiled. "To you anyway."

I tried to bite down on my grin. I couldn't expect him to be sorry for the irritation he'd caused Chevelle with his advances on me. Besides, Chevelle had thrown him across the room and into a wall. I was pretty sure they were even.

"It was Asher," I said. Our slow pace came to a halt as Steed turned to me. I wasn't sure why I'd said it, probably because of the fresh memories brought up earlier. All that had come back to me the last few weeks. But once I'd started, I couldn't seem to stop. "He found out."

Steed placed his hands on my arms in a comforting gesture.

"I'd hidden it from him. I knew I must. But he figured it out." I drew a quick breath. "He used it against me. He decided to take Chevelle for his own purposes. It would keep me in line." A harsh laugh escaped. If he'd only known. "I hadn't realized he'd caught on. I thought it was a banquet, a show of power, just like any other. But the room was crowded and he had me in a gown, not the clothes of a warrior. I stood beside him, his second." I could still see Asher as he moved to silence the crowd. I shook my head. "When he announced the arranged marriage, all my training vanished and I couldn't stop myself from finding Chevelle across the room. You should have seen his face."

I looked into Steed's dark eyes. "I couldn't let him. I stepped forward and refused." I took another shallow breath. "I denied him. For everyone."

Steed was speechless. I had meant for him to be released of guilt. There was no one who knew the truth of it but us. Steed couldn't have but believed it to be fact. But I could see my explanation had only made it worse.

"Later," Steed asked, "when Sapphire was taken?"

"Yes, I decided to run with him. And they killed his mother." I tried to keep the shame from my voice.

Steed pulled me against him and we stood in silence. My cheek pressed to his chest, I finally breathed deep. I had never spoken of it. I couldn't have. But Asher was gone now.

I was so wrapped up in thought, I didn't realize the sound was advancing footsteps until Chevelle stepped around the corner. And then, when Steed shifted, I was struck by the fact that we were locked in an embrace.

Apparently, Steed had shifted to see who was approaching, because his arms dropped from my back and his chest slid away. I hung there for a moment, watching Chevelle's frozen form at the end of the corridor.

Steed cleared his throat. I straightened. Both of us resisted the urge to explain it was not what it looked like.

I wasn't positive how long the three of us stood so, but it seemed like an incredibly long moment before Steed's mouth quirked.

"Well," he said, "I'll see you in a bit, sunshine."

I turned just in time to catch him wink at me and casually continue down the corridor in the direction we'd been heading.

He began whistling a tune and I could only be thankful it was the opposite direction from Chevelle.

We stayed frozen for an eternity, and then I picked up Steed's cue and smiled at Chevelle, as if everything were completely normal. "Hungry?"

He finally opened his mouth to answer, but the clatter of metal on stone caused us both to pause. When no other sound followed, I waited for Chevelle to respond, his hearing superior to mine. I held my breath until he rushed toward me, and then I spun to catch him on his way past. He was heading for the noise, and he didn't look happy.

5

PRETENDER

As we ran, it occurred to me Chevelle was holding back. I was far from able to keep up with him when he was at full speed. What I didn't know was whether he was setting the pace to stay with me, as my guard, or if whatever he'd heard wasn't such an immediate threat. We met Rhys and Rider in the corridor and the four of us turned into the dining area to find Steed, sword to the neck of a small male elf on the stones before him.

The scene made me pause, as I'd not seen Steed use a sword, and then I realized the clanking metal would have been this elf's sword hitting the stone floor where he now lay, arms bent behind him as if he planned to crawl backward, away from the very intimidating dark elf. I was a little proud of my guard. Steed looked quite impressive at the moment.

Steed didn't take his glare off his captive when he said, "Bind him."

"Done," Chevelle answered.

Without turning, Steed tossed the sword back for Chevelle, who caught it by the base of the blade and did a cursory examination of the handle. Steed grabbed the prisoner by his arm and hefted him up to walk beside us as we crossed to a more secure location.

Two doors down, Rhys and Rider were posted outside as Steed tossed the elf into a chair and bound him to it. Chevelle sealed the room. They did quick work and I simply stood in the center of the room to stare at this strange character. He wore nondescript clothing, no markers of any kind. His hair was muted brown. He definitely did not have the look of a light elf, not that inner glow or glistening eye, but he didn't appear to be of the northern clans either. He was young. And he looked scared.

"What's this?" Chevelle asked, beside me.

"I am not exactly clear on that," Steed answered. "But it seems he has some business with our lord."

Chevelle threw the sword at the elf's feet. I could feel the anger roll off of him, but his tone was smooth. "Business?"

Arms bound, stuck in a chair, the prisoner lifted his chin defiantly. Both Steed and Chevelle took a step forward. He swallowed as he gathered his courage. "Bring me to her," he demanded. Neither man glanced back at me.

So he didn't know who I was. Then what was he doing here?

"What do you want with her?" Chevelle's voice was deadly and I could only imagine the glare that accompanied it.

"I will see the pretender," he hissed.

Well, that was telling. I elbowed past my guard and leaned toward him, showing him my eyes.

The green was pretty effective. He was speechless. I was confident we would break him, so the small silver blade that materialized in an instant and shot toward me caught me completely off guard. Instinct caused me to turn, but as I rolled away from the dagger, it sliced the meat of my shoulder.

I spun, landing in a defensive crouch, just in time to see the fatal blow Chevelle landed on the young man. Danger thwarted, both men turned to me.

"What was that?" I yelled. They stared at me. "Did he just pull silver out of the air?"

They reacted to my words then, eyes landing first on my arm, which was now wet with blood, and then to the floor behind them.

A flat shard of metal lay on the stone. Chevelle's gaze returned to me, but Steed's went back to the chair. Rhys and Rider were suddenly there, struggling to take in whatever had happened.

Chevelle moved toward me and I became aware I was near panting. I straightened and slowed my breathing, hands and thighs still tingling with adrenaline. He examined my arm as Steed picked up the sword at the feet of the corpse. Steed appeared thoroughly confused as his gaze returned to the blade on the floor behind him.

Feeling returned to my arm and I jerked, but Chevelle had a tight grip. "It is a clean wound," he informed me. He bound a strip of fabric around it to stop the bleeding and instructed Rhys to find Ruby.

Chevelle turned. "Rider, this was an attempt on Elfreda." No one missed that he'd used my official name and each in the room tensed, myself included. "We know nothing, but can assume he did not travel alone." Chevelle's tone deepened to something resembling an animal. "Find them."

Rider disappeared from the room without another word and then Ruby was in the doorway. She had some choice words for the scene, but attended my injury.

Steed was standing over the offending blade and now that I

was taken care of, Chevelle joined him. They didn't seem to want to touch it. Ruby was pestering me with questions and poking at the gash in my arm, so I didn't catch what they were saying. I stood to join them. My head spun a little and Ruby protested wildly, but she followed me, working as we went.

Steed glanced at me. "It doesn't seem to be the same metal."

"What does that mean?" I asked.

"He didn't pull the element from anything on him. I checked him myself. If it wasn't the sword..." He trailed off.

"How is that possible?" Ruby asked.

No one answered. There was no answer.

Chevelle straightened to face me. "What did it look like?"

I was confused for a moment, but realized neither he nor Steed would have been able to see it from their vantage point. I had a feeling neither was happy that I'd pushed past them and stuck my nose in the attacker's face. "It was quick. Smooth but not liquid. His eyes were connected with mine and he never lost focus. There was nothing, and then silver." I sighed. "I'm not even sure I realized it was a blade until I was moving."

Ruby glanced at the chair. "Who bashed his skull?"

Steed and I gave Chevelle matching accusatory glares. He didn't budge.

"Well, we'll never find anything out now," she complained. "What do you suppose he wanted?" Her gaze flicked to my shoulder. "Aside from Frey."

Chevelle really didn't like fairies. I answered to save her. "He must have been put up to it."

"He snuck through the kitchens," Steed put in. "There's no way anyone with knowledge of the castle would have sent him that route."

"Did he say anything else?" I asked. "When you found him, what did we miss?"

Steed shrugged. "He immediately demanded to see you, sword drawn." He met my gaze with a kind of apology. "I had no idea he was a threat. He seemed so weak."

I waved it off and looked back at his lifeless form. It didn't seem possible. "He's just a boy."

"No one of note helped him," Chevelle said. "They would have waited."

The banquet. Why hadn't he attacked tonight, when I would have been vulnerable? He could have walked right up to me and had done with it in front of every clan leader. "Was he a warning?" Unease filtered through the group. "Maybe he was never meant to succeed?"

"But the silver," Steed said, shaking his head.

"Maybe he thought he was strong enough to do it. The talent made him special where he was from so he decided he would just raid the castle," Ruby suggested. "Where *is* he from, by the way? He doesn't look right."

"We didn't find out," I answered, and we all looked at Chevelle again.

Still nothing.

Grey came in, a wild energy lighting his face. I'd seen him quick before, but never on task. It made a difference. "Witnesses saw a similar youth matching the description come in with the deliveries. He seems to have been working alone, as he was unaware of a few customs and didn't appear to have a purpose. No one accosted him, they presumed it was merely due to inexperience. We would like to confirm his identity with the witnesses."

Chevelle nodded. "Very well, but keep him from anyone else's sight. Resume the search within the castle and surrounding the gates, but only until the guests begin to arrive. I want no one to know what has happened here."

6

BANQUET

As I lay back in the tub, letting the warm water ease the strain caused by the morning's events, my mind kept returning to the dull eyes of the boy who'd nearly killed me.

It had been so close. I'd been exceptionally stupid. In a matter of hours, I would be facing every figurehead in the north. I could not make the same mistake. I would have to make my position clear, leave no doubt. The banquet might be my last chance.

I sank lower into the tub, allowing the water to soak my patched-up wound. It burned horribly and I closed my eyes, letting the pain sear my memory, keeping it as a reminder of what my slip could have cost me.

A muffled click came from the door but I didn't bother looking. "Ruby, get out of my washroom."

She huffed. "How do you always know it's me?"

I turned to glare at her over the rim of the tub. "Because no one else would hassle me here."

"Hmm." She dropped something on the counter and turned to go. "I was simply bringing some things you'll need for this evening. I have to prepare myself as it is."

When the door shut behind her, I tilted my head back again, contemplating a display of power that would cement my place. I recalled a few of Asher's triumphs, but most of those disgusted me. He considered his banquets a success if each of his guests left in fear. He used his power as a threat, constantly reminding those around him of the damage he could do. He'd explained to me privately that he had to, it was the only way to secure our rule. But I knew better. I knew because he'd used it against me, and I'd had no desire for reign.

Asher had known me better than I'd known myself. No matter how I played along with his games, he'd kept me under his power, showed me what he could do. When I'd strayed, he'd found ways to remind me. I could see Chevelle again, his tortured form writhing in pain. At the hand of his own father. No matter his end, I still hated Rune. He had smiled as Chevelle lay before him. Chevelle had refused to call out, but his body had reacted against his will, his jaw clamped tight, muscles bucking against the stone floor.

Anvil had stepped in to save us that day, but I'd vowed it would happen no more. I'd made a demonstration of my own. But Asher had always been one step ahead of me. What had happened to Sapphire hadn't been punishment for my defiance, it had been a device to keep me. And it had worked. When I'd seen her lifeless body, getting out had no longer been an option. I had to stay and overcome Asher. I could not have done otherwise.

My mother had known that. She had seen, even from her prison, that it was reaching a boiling point. She had thought to save me. And she had burned for it.

I sighed and rose from the tub. A trail of water ran from my feet, tracing the seams of the stone floor. I pushed it with magic, testing the new powers once more. It moved as if a gentle wind blew. I was pleased, but not quite confident enough to dry myself, so I used a towel, just in case.

Since returning to the castle, I'd moved into one of the suites. From the washroom, there was a wardrobe closet through the first door, and a bedchamber beyond the second. As I walked through, I picked up the small bag of items Ruby had left me and glanced inside. She was incorrigible. I sat it aside and sifted through the various costumes hung along the back wall. I pushed aside a dark cloak and faltered when the long white gown came into view. My mother's wedding dress. I ran a hand over the beading, exploring the fabric, the detail.

But, no, this wasn't the dress. It had burned when she had burned. This gown had been created by Junnie. It was a symbol. A warning to Council.

Because of my mother, that white dress had become legend among the light elves. It had given the stories that indefinable something, had even made them appealing enough for the fairies to repeat. Not that I'd ever heard them. Bound as I was, the villagers would never have dared reveal anything of my past. But I had heard since I'd been back. And I understood.

Junnie had left me that dress when Council had decided to try me. They'd intended to imprison me, and Junnie had sent them a grave reminder.

And the crystal necklace. It had no real power, but it had frightened the Council leaders unreasonably. I guessed that was a kind of power of its own. Just a token, that was all it took.

An idea for the banquet was finally forming. I nodded as I slid into a pair of black leather pants, adjusted my top to cover the wound on my arm, and laced up my boots. I would not wear the armor over my injured shoulder, so I opted for wrist cuffs and seated a light cape into the shoulder clasps fashioned after hawks. I would be a warrior this evening, and I would look the part.

I began to step into the next chamber, but stopped. I hadn't wanted most of what Ruby had left for me, but there was one thing that might prove useful.

I slid a small canister from the bag, lining my eyes with gloss black, nearly the exact shade as my hair and lashes. It highlighted the green perfectly. *One of a kind*, I thought. And then smirked, as Ruby sported her own set of green eyes as well. Let them think of that.

I strapped on my sword and headed for the study to meet the others.

Grey, Anvil, and Steed were waiting for me, each decked out in their castle finery. Steed and Grey had yet to get used to the formal gatherings, but they definitely looked the part. Leather and silver adorned their upper bodies, weapons at hip and back. They were strong, and though Grey appeared lean next to Anvil's mass, the group somehow felt unified. Steed wiggled his eyebrows at my appearance. I ignored him.

"What news?"

"The witnesses have confirmed the identity of the intruder," Grey reported. "Due to the banquet, we have been unable to gather more information regarding his route to the castle, but once here, he'd not been linked to anyone."

"Has anyone of note refused the invitation?"

"No," Anvil answered. "All are anxious to bear witness to the new power they have heard of, or to see you fall." He smiled.

"I would imagine," I said. "No change, then. We will proceed as planned."

Steed and Grey did a little salute of sorts at my command, the shuffle of their boots on stone bringing my attention to their straightened posture. I shook my head at their dutifulness.

"To the hall."

As with the throne room, there was a private entrance to the hall, designed to allow direct access to the designated position without having to navigate the crowds. Asher hadn't liked to be touched. Still, it was a good idea and also handy for making a grand entrance.

Chevelle was waiting for me there. I had the pleasure of seeing his jaw go tight at my arrival, but was quickly distracted by his own getup. He had been raised wearing the garb of a warrior and it fit him well. It had been a very long time since I had seen him so, and I'd forgotten exactly how well. I cleared my throat.

"Elfreda." He nodded formally.

"Vattier," I threw back, and irritation took over as his chief emotion. I could deal with that. The other was too distracting.

He reviewed the arrangements for the evening before asking, "Have you made your decision on the demonstration, or are you still planning to… wing it?"

I didn't bite. "I have a fully choreographed performance. Not to worry."

He looked dubious. We stood there for a moment, knowing a full hall awaited us, but neither eager to proceed. He would not be at my side through the evening, as Asher had spent many years planting seeds of distrust and prejudice against Chevelle to prevent any alliance on my part. My public denial of him had done nothing to help matters, either. As it was, the position he held as my guard was generating plenty of whispers.

Chevelle stepped forward, his hand on my waist, and my pulse stuttered for an instant. But he spun me around, speaking low as he did so, explaining, "Checking your wound. No one must see this." He adjusted the material, verifying everything was still in place, and spun me once more to face the door as he stood behind me. His hands ran the edge of my cape to settle on the bare skin of my upper arms and he leaned in to murmur, "Show them who you are."

His breath on my ear caused a shiver and then his hand found my lower back and gave a little push toward the door. I didn't look back when I heard a low chuckle.

And I was so glad we'd called "even" earlier, because I was about to tip the scales.

The hall fell silent the moment I entered. They had been waiting on my arrival, but no doubt it didn't hurt that all the servers stopped what they were doing and turned to the dais. I stopped for a moment to find each of my guard (excepting Ruby) scattered about the room, purposefully not acknowledging the presence of any leaders. I'd had a gathering previously, but not of this magnitude, and many were left out intentionally, so I continued as if no other event had occurred.

"As the former guard is disbanded"—a reminder that we'd killed them—"I have invited the clans to gather"—a reminder they were here upon invitation—"to honor the seven of my new guard."

These men were no fools. They had watched my eyes fall upon only six men. There would be a building curiosity to the identity of the seventh. I nodded toward the steward and service began. It was a brief speech, but there was more to come.

I stepped from the dais and took my seat at the head of the table to feast among the leaders of the north. The room was furnished not like the dining area with its long, narrow tables, but with many short tables, arranged so that my slightly elevated position became the focus of the room, as well as the dais behind me.

Anvil had positioned the attendees in order of preference; two elderly men who had supported me throughout sat on either side, progressively going to people less supportive and more troublesome, all the way to downright dangerous. That meant most of the rogue clan leaders were across the room, and I avoided their stares as I was served. I raised my glass to the air and toasted, "The Seven," before bringing it to my lips, the scent of oak and spiceberry hanging in wait. Rhys and Rider's gazes took in those who did not join in.

A feast was served, and as instructed, the wine flowed at an increasing rate. Soon, the hall was loud with conversation, banter, and debate. Those near me, thanks to Anvil's design, did not speak of much, so I was able to catch bits of various discussions throughout the room. In an attempt to disguise my focus, I let my eyes fall on the immense tapestries insulating the cool stone walls, most adorned with images of my crest and a variety of innocuous scenes, as Ruby had removed any in tribute to Asher. In truth, she had had any evidence of him that could feasibly be removed taken from the grounds and burned. The castle was pretty bare at the moment. But torches, candles, ridiculous centerpieces, and elaborate dishes seemed to be more than adequate cover, in this room at least.

The clansmen were more at ease, loosing their armor, shedding cloaks, leaning back in their chairs, sated with food, wine, and talk.

Sudden warmth against my palm stole my focus, the signal from Ruby. I looked down to find the napkin under my hand had caught fire, but I was able to snuff it out before anyone noticed. I made a mental note to be more specific with the details next time.

I straightened in my chair just in time to see her enter. I gasped, but the slip went unnoticed in the noise. It was fortunate, as an instant later the hall fell silent. I'd not expected her to follow through so absolutely.

I gave them a moment to take in what I'd seen. A petite fairy, covered from chest to toe in slim black leather, arms bare but for wrist cuffs, belted with short, shiny knives, and donning the crest of the guard at her collar. The brown leather whip at her hip had been exchanged for polished black, with what appeared to be silver spikes at the tip. Her heeled boots were gone, as she'd laced into the flat guard issue. Her face was unpainted and impassive. All that remained of the familiar Ruby was the blazing red hair that curled feral around her, proclaiming her fey.

Before anyone had a chance to regain themselves, I stood, raising my glass to Ruby. "Now that we are all present, let the festivities begin."

One more breath of stunned silence was all that remained before the hall erupted into protest. I drank the toast, but didn't see whether any of my guard partook, because my eyes were still on the fairy guard. She watched only me, not the crowd, and I smiled at her. I couldn't help it.

So far, I thought I was off to a pretty good start.

7

INFERNO

The room was near chaos, which probably meant that Ruby was happy.

I wasn't sure how long to give the disorder before proceeding to the next step, but the display received a stronger reaction than I'd planned, and it was gaining momentum. Maybe we'd served too much wine. I sat, contemplating my next move, and the crowd settled a bit. One of the guests stood, and I realized they'd only quieted to hear his confrontation. With me.

I leaned forward in waiting, not surprised to find it was Rothus.

He was tall and broad, nearly as large as Anvil. His black hair was long, slicked back into a braid. He wore a cape of fur and a pegged mallet hung at his waist. He had plenty of magic, but he preferred blunt force. I nearly winced at the thought of what he'd likely done to the animal whose pelt covered his shoulders.

"You dishonor these grounds with a fey whore."

Ooh, that would do it. I stood to meet his gaze. "You challenge my decision?"

All sound ceased but the flickering of torchlight.

Rothus was a prideful man who held grudges. He hated fey as they hated iron. What I didn't know was whether he held that hatred above his current existence. The silence keyed him in on his mistake and he pushed his chair back to take a knee, but he didn't exactly recant. "They have no place among us."

"As you have no place to dispute the pronouncement of your lord." I paused for a heartbeat, and then, "Guard, acquire your price."

I sat, my obligation resolved.

From my periphery, I saw Grey flinch and feared he would intervene. I'd not thought to gauge his response to Ruby's appearance or the risk she was about to take. It was a mistake on my part, and I added it to the list. But Steed caught him with a gesture so minute, I was confident no one else saw it. Besides, they were all watching the fire fairy in guard's garb cross the room to her target.

Wearing a blank expression, Ruby walked coolly through the crowd to stand behind Rothus. On bended knee, he was nearly as tall as she and I was grateful he'd shown at least that respect. She pulled a dagger from her waist and grabbed hold of his braid. The whole of the hall tensed until a swift move sliced the braid and a crop of black hair fell forward around his face. It was insulting, but far from what the other guests had expected. Without a word, she walked back to her place, a firm grip on the dagger in one hand and braid in the other.

I'd given none cause to dispute the action, and the fact that Ruby hadn't used fire in her revenge might keep her heritage from the topic when the story was repeated.

Another round of wine was served and the crowd eventually settled into the din of conversation.

I had decided to give them a bit longer before the display of power when an exchange caught my attention. Dagan of Camber was a little too far in his drink, speaking noisily of "before." Dagan had clout. He held dominance over many here, and some believed fear of his power had kept the region from going completely lawless in my absence. I wanted no conflict with him, but his words were irritating me unreasonably. I resolved to go ahead with the next step to shut him up. And that was when it all went out the window.

Looking back, it was hard to recall exactly what he said that caused my anger to explode. Something about Chevelle that went right through me. What happened next would likely be repeated through history.

I'd only intended to shatter the cup in front of him, just to get his attention. Instead, a deafening blast sounded as every cup on every table in the entire hall burst into pieces at once, sending shards of pewter and glassware flying to clink against walls, splinter into tables, and generally shower down on everything, excepting myself. The fact that I was staring at Dagan clued everyone who'd not heard his comments in on the cause.

The room fell silent once again and the drip of wine from table and stone seemed amplified by it. Red splattered my guests as if they had attended a massacre and not a feast. The final few who were still taking in the scene came to join the others in their gawking at me.

I realized I was standing, which I couldn't remember doing. My own wineglass sat undisturbed, my person and all that surrounded me in an arm's length radius untouched by the destruction that blanketed the rest of the hall.

There was no question I had instilled fear in them. My task

was complete and I didn't have much taste left for festivities. I leaned down, lifted the glass in salute to my guard, and turned to walk from the room.

When I reached the corridor, I allowed myself to breathe again. I walked toward the study, thinking of the faces of my guard, sprayed red and numb with shock. I kept walking, past my chambers, past the commonly used rooms, up the stairs and out the window to my perch on the roof. The wind was cutting, but I stood to face it.

"Tell me that wasn't your plan," Chevelle said from behind me.

I choked on a laugh. I'd been standing in the wind so long my eyes watered and my nose and cheeks burned. I turned to look at him, relieved to find him clean and out of uniform. He untied his cloak and stepped up behind me on the small platform. When he reached around to blanket me with the cloak, the warmth felt so good I held his arm to wrap around me. I felt him relax into the embrace and I snuggled my face into the cloak to thaw. I breathed in his scent and then straightened, hoping he hadn't noticed.

"I had a good plan," I said as we stared out into the night. An agreeable rumble vibrated in his chest. It reminded me of a purring cat and I smiled. "I don't suppose it matters now."

"They were convinced," he assured me.

Chevelle wasn't like me. He possessed a nearly unshakable calm and considerable patience. After all we'd been through, there was no question he would have taken revenge on Asher. Everyone knew that. What they couldn't guess was the backlash it would cause. What traps Asher had set for him. If he were to fail, what that would have meant for me. If he were to succeed, what that would have meant for the realm. Chevelle had understood that. He'd kept me from acting rashly, a reckless vengeance that would have likely gotten me killed. I would have retaliated with passion. He could wait.

And he was right. There was a difference between courage and suicide. Honor wasn't much good to the dead.

"Chevelle?"

"Hmm?" he purred. I shivered. He could think it was from cold.

"How did you know I'd kill Asher?"

He stiffened. "We didn't."

I felt my face contort, but couldn't decipher what they'd actually planned when we'd confronted him among his guard.

Chevelle sighed. "When we found that he'd set bindings on you, we had to allow him to live."

They'd made a deal.

"He'd been collecting new powers. He'd learned to create a binding that would not release upon his death."

Which explained why Chevelle had been studying bindings instead of just hunting the Council.

"When Council attacked your mother, it set so much more into motion. Francine was to be taken, and you, but Junnie stepped in. She forced their hand with an arrangement no one could refuse by Council law. Council bound you both, for their safety, and permitted you to live. Under their watch."

"I can't remember," I said. "I remember everything else. But not the bindings. Was it long?"

"No, the entire process was very quick. When Council descended, Asher set his spell and ran. And then you were gone." He faltered, then corrected. "In the village."

I had been gone. And it had seemed a very long time.

"He watched you, to be certain you weren't affected by the castings. Apparently, he saw enough of your old self there to approve. Once Council was disposed of, we expected him to release you. He wanted you back as his second, under his control."

"So, when I stabbed him…"

"Not exactly the plan."

"Wow."

A short strangled laugh escaped him, the kind mingled with relief and disbelief. We sat in silence for a few moments, recalling Asher's last words. The words that would release the bindings. The words that would direct his power to me. If it hadn't been for some messed-up sense of pride on his part, I'd still be bound. Trapped in my own mind. Or dead.

"There is something you should know, Frey."

I waited.

"Junnie saved your life. She protected you. She fought for you."

"But?"

"We are not certain she meant to keep Asher alive long enough to unbind you."

I nodded, forcing myself to ignore the tightness in my chest. "All right." I took a deep breath. "But she's still done nothing to warrant my enmity." There was no way to prove she had intended to keep me bound now. Though it was possible. If nothing else, she might have only been trying to keep her family alive. How many of the Council members who were slaughtered had been her blood?

Fannie had been responsible for many of those deaths. Junnie had saved her, and Fannie, as she escaped her bonds and regained pieces of her old self, had slipped into madness, reaping revenge on those who had trapped her. She had cut down her own family, Junnie's family. My family. A small voice whispered that as a result, Council's resistance to Junnie was now shrunk by half, but I choked it off. Fannie was dead. Asher was dead. Junnie was all that was left.

I sighed and turned from Chevelle's embrace to face him, handing his cloak back. "I'd like to meet with the guard in the morning."

He stepped back and gave a curt nod, and it made me feel as horrid as I was being.

8

EXCURSION

They were scattered about the study, patiently waiting for me. It still annoyed me I was the only one who needed so much rest. Ruby's hair was pulled back, exposing the points of her ears. Not entirely fey, but close enough.

"What news?" I asked before they had a chance to take their places at the table.

Anvil reported. "Word has already flooded the valleys. There were but a few minor protests south of Camber. No news of the reaction of the rogues."

"We will ride out today. Silence the dissidents." A few eyebrows rose. "Grey, Chevelle, Rhys, with me." I glanced at Steed. "Ruby will need to lie low for at least three days. Please attend her." I wasn't finished, but Ruby was bloodying her lip waiting to respond. I let her.

"Three days?"

"One for word to reach the outlying camps. One for them to form a plan. One to implement it. If they do not strike by then, they will not bother. At which point, and only then, will you be allowed free rein."

Her eyes narrowed on me and I decided to nip the rest of my fairy problems in the bud.

I turned to Grey. "Until the fourth day, she will be Steed's charge." He looked like I'd slapped him. "You put us all at risk last night, but none more than Ruby. Had you stepped in to protect her, she would have no power. When we return, you will lead a scouting mission for information on the boy. Someone will have seen him or his silver." And I would need to find the wolves.

Mention of the assassin had brought a stillness to the room. I struggled for a way to express my thanks to this group that meant so much to me. They had brought me back from nothing, had risked their lives for this. Everything seemed inadequate, but the silence was growing too loud.

"You have done us proud."

Grey and Rhys were mounted and waiting at the gate when I reached the stable. Chevelle stood outside, holding the reins of both horses. It seemed like people were always waiting on me. I picked up my pace.

Chevelle handed my reins over with a wry smile. "Your Steed."

I bit my cheek at the name I'd given my horse and swung up into the saddle as quick as Chevelle. Side by side, I replied in a hushed tone, "I am surprised you've let me keep him."

The smile dropped from his face. "Yes. Well, I considered replacing him. But, in truth, he is one of the nicest mounts in the land." He winced at his own words and kicked his horse up to gallop.

I swallowed a laugh and joined him.

87

We were quiet as we made our way from the castle. When we'd cleared any foot traffic, Grey and Rhys rode ahead as sentries.

I still felt guilty about berating Grey so publicly.

Chevelle saw me watching. "You wounded his honor."

"It was right."

He eyed me knowingly before returning his gaze to the mountain. "I heard what Dagan said."

I flinched. "That doesn't mean I wasn't right."

He didn't respond.

Leave it to Chevelle to stand up for him. It was hardly the same thing.

It was my first outing since our return from Asher's lair. Any of the guard could have made this demonstration, but I'd wanted to see the mountain myself. The dark rock had been my home, these pathways my playground. I wanted to see what had changed, what had been lost. I needed to know how I would be received by them all, not just the clan leaders.

After the massacre, there had been no one in control. It had been known Asher had lived and though he had been in hiding, I supposed fear of his return had been heavy in the minds of those who might take advantage. I, as his second, would have been regent if not in hiding of my own. As it was, neither of us ruling but neither confirmed dead, the goings-on had continued day by day. The staff had cared for the castle, the grounds, completed their tasks as usual. No one wanted to lose their positions, let alone their lives, if Asher were to reappear.

He might have been a harsh ruler, leading by fear and control, but he was Lord. He was respected. He was obeyed. Now that he was gone, his half-breed granddaughter who had never wanted to rule didn't quite strike fear into the hearts of her people. And there was only one thing they hated more than fairies. Humans.

Over the last few weeks, I'd realized it was fortunate the way things had worked out. We could have died a thousand ways by now, Chevelle and I, as we went for revenge in the grasp of rage. Nothing short of losing every memory I had could have kept me from settling scores. And nothing short of recovering me could have kept him from doing the same. I had taken care of Asher. Chevelle had seen me returned. Now one objective remained. And I would stay alive long enough to see it through if it was the last thing I did.

"You look like you're trying to memorize something," Chevelle said.

"You look like a member of the royal guard," I retorted.

His eyes narrowed on me.

I shrugged.

And suddenly, we were flying through the air. For half a second, I thought Chevelle had retaliated, but there was nothing playful about the hit I'd taken. I hadn't even seen him come off his horse, but he'd slammed into me at full speed. We came to an abrupt stop as we smashed into the rock beside the path. Chevelle rolled into a crouch as I lay there, staring at the sky. The impact had knocked the wind out of me. A screaming pain in my side accompanied the return of my breath, but instinct kicked in and I was on my feet again, crouched beside Chevelle.

Our horses were gone, the clatter of their hooves fading as I listened. Rhys and Grey were across the path, a few lengths ahead, eyes scanning the mountain. It was obvious I'd missed something, and it didn't look good. Beside me, Chevelle was searching as well. I sank to my knees and closed my eyes.

A falcon nested in the branches of a thorn tree not far from where we hunkered. I set it to flight, ignoring the metallic tinge of blood in my mouth.

Nothing. Everything looked right, normal. Nothing out of place, no danger. I released the bird and opened my eyes. I glanced over to find Grey and Chevelle in the middle of an exchange of silent gestures across the distance. I'd clearly missed most of it, but they had lost my attacker.

My head snapped up to find Chevelle. His grim expression confirmed what I'd thought I'd seen pass between them. I'd been attacked. Again.

His head tilted toward the ground behind us. Several yards away lay what looked to be a shard of glass.

"No," I hissed.

Chevelle nodded. There was only one thing that created weapons like that. *Ice fairy*.

We both stepped closer to the offending splinter of ice. It was formed solid, nearly unbreakable, and almost impossible to see coming at you. I shook my head. I hadn't even seen a fairy. I reached to pick up the icicle, disturbed by how much it reminded me of the silver dagger that had all but stabbed me, and Chevelle put a hand on my arm to stop me.

"It's not right," he whispered.

Obviously, I thought, and then I realized what he'd meant. It didn't smell right. There was a nasty, acidic tang to it. Poison.

Rhys and Grey were behind us now.

"Are you well?" Rhys asked.

They all waited while I took stock. "Yes."

Chevelle eyed my side; I hadn't been aware that I was keeping pressure against it. I dropped my hand, daring him to question it.

He didn't, instead dealing with the most pressing issue. "We should return to the castle."

For a moment, I considered going ahead with our agenda, but that would just be stupid. I nodded.

He stared at me for a moment. I stared back. He raised his eyebrows. Mine met the challenge. He sighed. "Frey, would you like to *ride* back?"

Oh. I bit my lip as I called the horses to us.

I stood silently watching my guard. Angry words flew through the study. Curses. Violent threats. No one had seen my attacker, a whisper of sound the only warning. No evidence remained but the sliver of ice. It lay on the table in a sealed container, frozen even now, in hopes that Ruby could discern the toxin. I couldn't breathe. I pulled shallow puffs through my nose. Anything deeper was a knife to my side. The ride back had nearly killed me. I was fairly positive something was broken.

Unexpectedly, they broke up and headed for the door. Chevelle lingered; I guessed he must have dismissed them. As the last noises faded in the corridor, he approached me.

"You've gone pale."

I nodded.

He smiled a little, glad I'd finally given. "Come, then." He walked me to my room and sat on the bed beside me, pulling my shirt aside to examine the injury. I raised my head to see, but as he pressed the skin, I fell back against the pillow with a gasp.

"Fractured rib, I think." He restored my shirt and patted my leg. "Hurts like a beast."

"The good news," I wheezed, "is I've barely thought about being assaulted again."

He looked as if he might be sick.

Someone cleared their throat at the open door and Chevelle's hand on my leg tightened. "I've asked Ruby to tend to you."

I glared at him.

He smiled and stood, leaving me to a special kind of torture.

Ruby had talked while she worked, trying to distract me to ease the pain. I'd refused her concoctions and she'd eventually left me to rest. But sleep wasn't coming. I lay staring at the canopy of the bed, building more and more anger as time passed.

Council had killed my mother. Murdered her in an attempt to suppress northern rule. Protection had been her blood right. My blood right. They had intended to take me, had only settled for my mind because of their own fear. No other threat would have been strong enough. Junnie had stepped in and used their superstition, their regard for the beast to quell their desire for domination. They had trapped me, held me prisoner, and when I'd finally been returned, I had been attacked again. In my own castle.

I couldn't know if that was Council as well, but the silver boy's hair was too light, his eyes too dull. He wasn't of the north. And if Council had never displaced us, none of this would have happened. I wouldn't have been riding out to control uprisings, and I wouldn't have been attacked yet again. *By fairies.* I bit down a growl.

"I've brought you some tea," Ruby announced from the door. I sighed, and the movement brought pain again.

She sat the cup on my table and took a chair beside the bed. I continued staring at the ceiling, because it hurt less to lie still. She didn't ask how I felt.

"While you were gone, I arranged some of your things," she said.

I didn't take time to speculate whether she'd been trying to annoy me, teach me a lesson for shutting her in the castle with a babysitter, or simply distract me.

"I've been wondering about something I found. The scroll."

I could see the words as plain as if they were before me now. *Fellon Strago Dreg.*

"I've looked everywhere. They are in no book that I have discovered."

My mother's script. A warning.

"I thought that maybe—"

Her words cut off as I stood, holding my breath to control the pain.

She stared at me.

"Ruby, gather the guard. We are going on a trip."

Her face was blank for a moment, but as I moved toward the closet, she walked from the room. I bit down hard as I pulled the shirt over my head and then replaced it with another, lacing a vest tight against my ribcage. I struggled into my boots and grabbed a cloak before heading to the study.

Ruby was fast. They were all there waiting for me. By the way they watched me, I thought she might have told them I'd lost it, but they were there.

"Prepare the horses," I said.

They stared at me.

"We ride out for Junnie."

The stillness of the room erupted into disorder. I raised a hand and they settled again.

"This is no coincidence."

"You think she would employ the fey?" Chevelle asked incredulously.

I shook my head. "I cannot be certain any of this is her doing. But we will find out."

"She has the most to gain," Ruby said.

"Junnie has done nothing but assist in Frey's return," Grey replied.

"As such, she would have aided herself," Rhys said.

"She wouldn't be able to raise a new Council with a lord who stood against her," Rider agreed.

I couldn't dispute that. Junnie might have merely seen me as the lesser of two evils. But I couldn't say I didn't feel the same way about her and this supposed new Council compared with the old.

"Did she not risk all when she saved Frey from the massacre?" Steed asked. "Was she not honoring her family? Defending their birthright? Why else would she have rescued Francine from the same fate?"

"Fannie could never have been truly saved," Chevelle answered.

It was true. Fannie had approached Council for protection, the only place left for her to turn. It had started something that she could not have anticipated, but none of that would have changed her outcome.

She had reaped her revenge on Council. But she had gone back to Asher, and she had paid for that with her life.

They continued the exchange, but it was nothing but useless speculation. The only one who hadn't voiced an opinion was Anvil. When the conversation died down, I looked to him.

He sighed, his large chest rising before falling in a defeated gesture. Anvil had been around for as long as I could remember, strong and solid. But as I watched him now, I could see the first signs of age on his face, the smallest creases around his eyes and mouth. He didn't want to tell me the last of my family could be my greatest adversary. But he was loyal. "Power can turn any."

It was the only answer I needed. "Mount up."

9

JOURNEY

We rode through Camber on our way, making no secret of our travels. The guard took formation, which would have been intimidation enough, but as we came through the southern encampments, we took the time to enforce our rule, make a show of our presence.

By nightfall, the ache in my side had become agonizing. When the vague outline of a structure came into view, I realized I'd stopped paying attention to my surroundings, simply riding along with the others. I was grateful to see the fort, downright rapturous when the horses came to rest. Chevelle was at my side, gingerly lifting me down, and the sense of relief was overwhelming.

We settled inside the walls, under an open sky, where Ruby had lit a nice fire. The warmth eased my muscles, tired from working to hold myself still against the jostling of the ride, and having a purpose improved my mood.

I finally glanced around the camp. Rhys and Rider had taken watch outside. They had informed me the wolves would remain at the castle, though I was unsure whether they'd not wanted to confront Junnie or whether they'd had some other purpose. The others relaxed around the fire. I was finally able to grasp that peculiar feeling that had been plaguing me all day. It was so like those odd memories from when I was bound. Days of riding, nights by the fire, these same faces watching me warily.

Chevelle saw the smile playing at the corner of my mouth from where he sat beside me. "Are we amusing?"

I laughed with a shallow huff. "Just remembering."

My eyes met his and he understood, but he didn't appear to find it humorous.

Ruby, however, picked up the conversation. "You were so funny, Frey." She tilted her head, deciding, and then, "But I still like you better now."

Grey snorted.

"I don't know," Steed said, "I think she was remarkably entertaining." He winked and I glanced down to hide my smile. He wasn't genuinely flirting now, he was only being Steed. But I was fairly positive his mere presence irritated the devil out of Chevelle.

"That was probably the abundance of fairy dust," I said pointedly to Ruby.

Her eyes narrowed on me. "I was trying to help you. I thought it would make it easier to find your memories. Or at least give you some relief." I felt almost guilty for a moment, until she smiled and added, "But it was fun to watch."

Grey made a comment about some ruckus she'd created by dusting an imp, but I wasn't listening. My gaze had fallen on Chevelle. He and Anvil were the only ones who had known me before, who had understood how truly lost I was, who had felt the full impact. Gone, Chevelle had said.

He saw my expression and met it with a sad sort of smile. "There were so many times we thought you were back." He shook his head. "I knew it wasn't possible, but still…" His brows pulled together, as if he were even now trying to work it out. "It was you."

I thought of the first day I'd seen him, outside Junnie's door. "I'm surprised you even recognized me under the blur of glamour."

He chuckled. "I heard you, stealing around the back of the house. You were about as stealthy as a bull elk in a boar's nest. Junnie tried to stop me. I wasn't supposed to be seen." But he'd been there, still and solid as a statue, and I'd nearly tumbled into him. "I suppose it was fortunate you were masked."

I remembered his face, the tightness in his muscles, the restraint apparent in every part of him. He'd turned from me with fisted hands and disappeared.

"And then you broke it," he continued. I glanced up at him, pulled from my reverie. "You stood before Council and transformed." He glanced at my hair. "Dark seemed to seep out, drowning the pale like oil over straw." His gaze moved to meet mine. "And your eyes shone as green as a fey flame."

I remembered. I'd unwittingly summoned the wind. Crushed the Council speaker's windpipe.

Chevelle laughed humorlessly. "I thought you were going to kill him right there. And then you just left."

I'd run.

I was unaware of how low our conversation had become, nearly a whisper, until rowdy laughter brought our attention back to the others. The banter between Steed, Anvil, and Grey had taken a fevered pitch, and they appeared ready to roll around the rock like tiger cubs. Ruby was egging it on.

"Yes," she taunted Anvil, "but you are more of a one-strike wonder." Grey and Steed were in an uproar at this, but she carried on. "Steed can outlast any man."

A snicker escaped me and she turned to us.

"Would you not agree?"

I bit my lip.

"Cursed fairies," Grey quipped, and there was suddenly a bolt of fire headed for his chest. He rolled and twisted and was abruptly standing behind her, hands at her hips. Her face was near the color of her hair and I laughed full out. She was going to slaughter him.

"He's quick," Chevelle said, shaking his head.

"You'd have to be." I smiled, indicating Ruby.

The exchange had evolved into a full-on brawl and Chevelle gave me a look that clearly implied it was my responsibility to manage it. Each day, I had more sympathy for what he must have endured on our previous journeys.

Steed tumbled over Grey and their boots landed in the fire, kicking up smoke and embers.

"Children," I commanded. I was reasonably certain they'd not even heard me. I tried again, standing for the order. "Cease."

Steed looked up from his place on the ground, cheeks smeared with dirt and ash, and quirked his brow. That sly grin was the only indicator that he was about to launch himself at me. I could say I had no intention of joining in the melee, but that would be dishonest. I was going to have a little fun with him.

I dropped to a defensive stance, arms out at the ready despite the ache in my side, just to give him permission. When he moved, I straightened back to my casual posture and waited. I let him get about halfway.

He was off his feet, airborne in his leap for me, when I flicked my wrist to leave no doubt where the blast had come from. I felt the percussion as it collided with his power, but it barely affected the strike. It threw him back with considerable force, which I expected, and into a very large boulder some distance from the camp, which I had not. The previously boisterous onlookers fell silent, not even laughing at Steed's shocked expression.

I might have overestimated the amount of power required for the move.

I hadn't meant to end our playtime so abruptly, but this was no time to admit it. I tilted my head slightly in acknowledgement, as if I'd not just humbled him in one motion, and turned back to my seat.

The smile I found on Chevelle's face could be called nothing but satisfied.

No one challenged me over the following days, but they didn't really spar either. I wasn't sure if the upcoming meeting was weighing down their moods, or if they were saving their energy. Either way, I didn't plan on practicing until I'd figured out control. I pledged to myself I'd find the wolves when we returned and work out how to share or store this extra energy before I hurt someone. And then I had to bite my lip not to smile at the memory of Steed's face when I'd sent him flying through the air.

"All right," Chevelle said as he brought his horse to a stop. "This is the nearest we can get you. We can wait for her to find us, or search for some clue of where she's hiding."

I smiled. "You make it sound as if she's——" My words cut off at a sound from the trees behind us. I turned to find Rhys and Rider entering the clearing.

They'd been following at a distance because I'd been attacked on our own lands. No one had expected this trip, so if there had been any other plotters, they'd be on the mountain. Not to mention that we didn't want any of the rogue clans pursuing us here, in the First Forests. Words forgotten, I scanned the surrounding trees.

I'd been surprised when Anvil had told me where Junnie would be. I wasn't exactly shocked she'd gone into hiding, considering she'd turned on her own Council and lost most of her family, but I hadn't expected her to stray so far north of the villages and forests that had been her constant. The trees here were thin and wiry, more needled than broadleaf. The forest floor was moss and ink-bristle. This was a palette of night blossoms and jade flower, not the sunny rainbow of her home. She'd feel out of place here. Cold.

I realized the others were watching me. Waiting.

"Set camp here. I'll have a look around. I should be able to tell where she's been." Surely, there would be some mark of her, some sign of growth or garden or change.

Ruby went straight to forming a large fire. I doubted we'd need to make a spectacle, it wasn't as if we'd be hard to spot, but I didn't spoil her fun. Rhys and Rider stayed close. I knelt, splaying my hands on my legs, and closed my eyes. I didn't expect to find Junnie so easily, but it was early afternoon, and I could at least get a feel for the land before she came to us.

I found a harrier and sank deep into its mind so I could cover a greater distance. It was easier with my own hawk, took less focus once I'd gotten familiar with its mind, but that was why I hadn't brought it. That familiarity allowed me to find it even now, back in the castle. It meant I could still keep an eye on things.

The forests were a striking green, dark patches among the clearings. The harrier took long, lazy circles and I could see the patches grow larger, taking over the clearings farther south. We weren't terribly far from the base of the mountain, closer to it than to any of Junnie's own people. It was a disturbing sign.

For a long time, I saw nothing out of the ordinary, no indication that she'd touched the land. But there was no hint of anyone else, either. It was simply wilderness, too far from anything. And then I saw a dog.

It wasn't mangy, in fact its coat was clean and shiny, a fluffy black that appeared to float about it as it ran. It didn't look as if it'd missed a meal either. I touched its mind briefly and knew. *Snickers.*

I came back to myself, shaking my head. They were watching me.

"She's there. A league or more from here, in a copse of blood oak."

Anvil glanced at the sky. Would we go now?

I nodded. If Junnie was behind the attacks, I didn't want to sit in wait.

"Do we go in mounted?" Steed asked.

"Yes. It's not as if we'll be able to sneak up on her." We could be stealthier on foot, but I was confident that by now she knew we were coming.

On Steed's command, the horses gathered and in moments the packs were secure and ready. Snickers was still running the field when we approached.

"Is that…" Grey trailed off as the dog spotted us and advanced, immediately picking up speed.

I answered a flat, "Yes," but the question on their faces was plain. How could he have grown so quickly? He was a giant, some terrifying mix of a mastiff and a wolfhound. I tried to work out his age in my head, but no amount of arithmetic could reconcile this massive beast with that puppy.

I tore my eyes away long enough to glance at Chevelle, whose expression was wary.

"Does he plan to eat us?" Anvil asked.

I managed a laugh. "No, but there will be slobber."

Ruby made some sort of disgusted noise and I turned to smile at her. Fairies didn't like dogs, and this one was bigger than she was.

We continued riding, though we could see the trees that framed Junnie's lodge. She'd formed the structure within the copse of blood oak, using the trees as column and canopy. Native ferns and mosses camouflaged it further and with the smattering of rock by the entrance, no one would have easily found her.

As we neared, she stepped from the trees in all her blonde glory. We stopped as a group and dismounted, and Snickers tested each of us, cold nose snuffling for our scent. Once finished, he chuffed and went to stand beside Junnie.

"He's grown quickly," I commented, though all of us knew it was unnatural.

Junnie smiled and I was struck, as I was each time I saw her, by how different we were. There was a lightness about her, shimmery golden hair, bright sky eyes, everything about her seemed to glow. It was made all the more perceptible by the new colors of her robes.

"I am glad you are returned, my Freya."

"Thank you, Juniper. I am grateful for all that you have done to help us."

Her gaze fell on the others. "Word of the Seven has traveled far. Even here, I have heard of their imposing presence."

I wanted to trust Junnie. I wanted to take her endearment and hold it in my heart, keep the last of my family, but I couldn't stop myself from questioning her words, couldn't keep from wondering who had told her of the guard, what she'd meant by imposing presence.

A silence hung in the air and then Anvil stepped forward, bowing slightly in greeting. "Juniper."

"Ah, Reed. Forgive me, it is simply such a shock to see Freya restored." She tilted her head to return his salutation and then smiled. "Alone for mere weeks and I've lost all trace of civilization." But she still didn't invite us in.

"Though I am certain Frey has been eager to see you," Anvil said, clearly struggling with the dictates of etiquette himself, "that is not the reason we have come."

Junnie straightened.

"She has been attacked."

Junnie's eyes flicked to mine, and I could tell she was concerned, but that ugly voice in the back of my mind wondered if she was worried for me or herself. I took a deep breath against the tight lacings of my vest and moved closer. "Twice actually."

She stared at me, waiting for more information. Or maybe an accusation.

"A boy entered the castle through the kitchens. Pulled silver from the air and formed a blade." I purposefully left off the fact that he'd managed to slice my arm and the details of his coloring.

"And then a second, outside the castle. It was in the form of an ice shard."

"Fey?" she asked, incredulous.

Ruby spoke up then. "There was a toxin within the crystal. I have been unable to identify its makeup, but it doesn't appear to be plant-based."

I started to turn back to Junnie, but Steed caught my eye. With the smallest glance, he conveyed his suspicion. By the time my eyes fell again on Junnie, I was just as wary. She was troubled, there was no doubt about that. But that wasn't what was bothering me. Why hadn't she invited us in? As they continued to discuss the attempts, I let my mind wander, trying to figure out what she could possibly be hiding. She should have wanted this meeting under cover.

And that was when I felt it. A human.

10

BETRAYAL

Before I could stop myself, I was past Junnie, pushing through the door. I could hear them all on my heels, but I didn't look back. I followed that strange feeling, that connection, through her house. Just before I threw open the last door, Junnie spoke my name. It was a cross between a plea and a command, and I ignored it.

On the back wall of a small, clean room was a crib.

I did look at her then. Her face held a hint of an apology, but not regret.

I opened my mouth, a thousand thoughts fighting for issue, but all that came out was, "Why?"

Junnie shook her head, what might have been sadness playing in her eyes. "I could do nothing else."

"You could do nothing else?" Anger and incredulity warred for my tone.

She sighed. "Asher chose this one above all others."

I stared at her for a long moment, her words repeating in my head. And then understanding came. A burst of power escaped in my fury as I turned back for the child.

"Hold!"

The words brought me up short. Rhys had never spoken anything but gently to me. This had been nothing short of an order. He stepped forward and tilted his staff past me. Where the grip touched, mere inches from us, the air rippled. There was a ward protecting the crib.

My teeth gritted as I glared at Junnie.

She was unrepentant. "I did not create this child, Freya. But she will not be destroyed."

My hand came forward, but Junnie was too fast. She stepped through the ward, cradled the babe against her chest, and burst out the back wall of the lodge.

Rage tore through me and the other walls surrounding us exploded into bits of kindling. My guard flinched, though most of the shards had flown outward. I took a breath. We could go after her, but we'd have to kill her to stop her.

I glanced at the others, and saw something like guilt on a few faces. I stepped forward, narrowing my gaze on Chevelle.

"We did not think it an issue."

I waited.

"The girl, Molly. It was clear she wouldn't survive to term."

I stood stock-still, certain if I moved at all, it would be to keel over and expel the contents of my stomach. I remembered Molly, the days she'd spent with us. She had irritated me inexplicably, though now I could see that it was likely because of my childhood, that constant conviction of my people that humans were detestable. And that we were the same, she and I, as alike as I was to the elves who surrounded me. She hadn't appeared with child to me. But she had been a human girl, and we had found her with the head of Asher's guard.

"You knew?"

Chevelle shook his head. "Ruby. The girl had gotten exceedingly ill."

I glanced at Ruby. She looked a little sheepish. I was finding it hard to breathe. My vest was too tight.

"No one expected her to make it," Chevelle continued, "and when Junnie showed up…"

"You didn't want us to kill her," Steed said.

"Junnie took the girl without asking," Chevelle put in, not sparing a glance for Steed. "But it did seem like an acceptable outcome." He shook his head. "I never thought she'd allow this."

"It was the child," Anvil said. "She said Asher chose this one. She will not destroy one who can connect with beasts. She will wait and see."

So Junnie thought the child might carry our ability. And those of the light were morally against destroying it. But there was no way to know. She was risking it merely because Asher had believed this one special.

No.

My stomach twisted at the thought. "She said above all others."

An image of the small bloodied hands came unbidden. The hands of a human girl. The ruined bodies of her and the guard in Asher's secret grotto near the castle.

"We believed them all destroyed," Chevelle assured me.

No one moved, and I had a sudden flash of memory from when I'd been bound, when they'd all thought at any moment I could lose it. "How many?" I asked.

"It is not known. Council, Junnie, your guard have each dealt with their own." His voice was gentle, and the "your guard" held a quiet assurance.

I didn't stop to ponder the details, to wonder if he and Steed had found more when searching for Asher's guard. There was something else more pressing.

"How long has he been doing this?" I searched the faces of my guard, but I had my own answer. He had taken Vita, had created Fannie and my mother, had stolen me.

"They're his." My voice met stony silence. "The others, the attacks. They are his."

"They are children," Anvil said. "They are not working alone."

He was right. But who had put them up to it?

We rode straight through the night, and barely rested the remainder of the journey. When we finally reached the castle, I fell into bed exhausted, but sleep still wouldn't come.

The attacks had been too odd, silver and ice. Though we'd not seen the source of the ice to be certain it wasn't fey, we had seen the boy. His features were too light, his eyes too dull. He had pulled silver from the air. He might have been old enough, might have believed he could defeat me, but why? What would he gain from it? It was easier to believe that the boy didn't hate me enough to want to kill me, but that he'd been after the throne.

Maybe he'd been abandoned. Maybe Asher had made promises and never returned. Maybe the boy had merely come for revenge, or because he had nothing left. And maybe not. The more likely scenario was that someone was still out there. Someone had told him he was the rightful heir. Someone had told him that I'd killed Asher, that all he needed to do was kill me.

Was it Junnie? Could she do this to me? Of course she could, she'd turned against Council, slaughtered however many of them. She'd had years of experience in underground maneuvers. By all accounts, she had plans to create a new Council. She had followers. But would she?

I found it hard to believe. I wanted to think it was true, that it wasn't emotion driving the conviction. But I had to look at the facts. Council had nearly destroyed the north. They had used my mother as a pretense in their bid for control. They'd been losing to Asher and they'd dealt with him. Junnie might have split from Council, but she still aimed for control. She might have preferred me on the throne to Asher, but there was no guarantee she didn't want to rule all. Junnie was a match for me in power, but now I had gained Asher's as well. It was my only edge, aside from my guard. But she could amass a Council larger than any of my forces. If you received the calling, you served. It wasn't a matter of free will or loyalty.

And then there was the child. Was Junnie truly keeping Asher's daughter because she felt it was wrong to do otherwise, or because it would be her ally, her key to the north?

I rolled over, kicking the bed sheets away. It could be the rogues. It could be the fey. It could be anyone. But I really didn't want it to be Junnie.

My thoughts turned to Fannie then, betrayed by her own father. He had essentially disowned her, choosing my mother over her as his second, and then me after he'd all but driven her insane. Fannie had turned to Council to protect them, as their birthright, and Council had betrayed them as well. She hadn't had someone to protect her as I had. When her bonds had begun to break, she'd thought Junnie and Council had entrapped her, and she'd gone for revenge. It had cost her life.

My thoughts floated in and out of those images, of Fannie razing the village that had been our prison, of the fires that had burned my mother. It was hard to say when they morphed into dreams, but I could see my mother in a gown of azure and lilac, leaning forward to whisper secrets.

"It was the bond," she said softly, "that was why my mother couldn't leave him."

"But——" I started, and her finger came up to silence me.

"It isn't right, my Freya. I cannot let him destroy her family so he might lay claim to more land."

And then she was burning. The flames licked at her white gown, beaded and lacy. Screams surrounded us, but I could hear her whispering, "Others will come. Others will come." The flames engulfed her and I was suddenly under water, struggling for air. *Others will come.*

I jerked awake, damp with sweat and panting. I lay staring at the ceiling, one thought circling through my mind like a bird over prey. *Others will come.*

I cursed Asher. He had made an army of his children, and they were going to come for me. One by one.

11

DECISION

Eventually, I accepted the fact that sleep would not be returning anytime soon, and dragged myself out of bed. I took a long bath before getting dressed, and let myself wince as I laced a corset around my ribcage. It was getting better, though, and I was able to take a few deep breaths before heading down to find the others.

I stepped into the hall and found Anvil leaning against the wall beside my room. I raised a brow.

"Only until we are certain," he answered.

I nodded. "It won't be long, I assure you."

He smiled a fiendish grin and I reached up to clap him on the back as we made our way down the corridor.

We found Ruby, Steed, and Grey in the dining area. When we sat to join them, I realized they were eating lunch, and wondered exactly how long I'd slept.

After two servings of braised elk and cornmeal, I decided I could face what I was going to have to do. "Find Rhys and Rider, we'll have a meeting as soon as everyone is gathered."

I excused myself and headed for Chevelle's study. He was

standing near the back wall, staring out the window. The silver dagger lay on his desk.

He turned and saw my focus. "It is an alloy."

I lost all awareness of my intention. "Alloy?"

He nodded grimly. "Yes."

"So…"

"So we have no idea the kind of threats we'll be dealing with. This and the ice——" He stopped when a note of anger slipped into his voice. "We will be fighting blind."

If I'd had any notion he'd forgiven Asher, it was gone. I was beginning to build on my own resentments as well. Even after Asher's death, I wasn't free from him.

Chevelle stared at me for a long moment. And then I realized I'd forgotten my purpose. "Oh. I've called a meeting."

He nodded and began to walk toward the door, but as he neared me, he saw there was more.

"I wanted to see you first," I explained.

His gaze fell to the hand fisted at my side, lingered, and then returned to meet mine.

"You trust me."

It wasn't a question, so he didn't answer. He simply waited for me to go on.

I didn't.

He came closer, reached down to take my fist in his hand, and loosened the fingers. I understood the gesture was meant to ease me, to let me know I could relax and just tell him, but it didn't have that effect. I fought the flush but forgot to mask my expression.

He moved even closer and released my hand so nothing stood between us but a few inches of air. I dropped all emotion from my face.

Chevelle's jaw tightened in response. "Do you know the one thing I enjoyed?" he asked, reaching up to cup my cheek.

I could only manage a quiet, "What?"

His thumb brushed my lip and the flush returned, despite my best efforts. "You couldn't hide it," he whispered.

I took a deep breath, reining it in as the memories rolled over me. Every look, every touch. "Well," I said, working for a steady tone, "you weren't doing so well yourself."

A sexy smile took over his face. "Still, it was"—his eyes fell to my lips, slowly tracing their line—"satisfying."

That was it. I'd finally made a good decision and I was going to cave after one touch from him. One word.

Ruby cleared her throat from the doorway.

I turned to her, stepping away from Chevelle, and couldn't decide whether to be angry or relieved at the interruption.

She looked a bit concerned for her safety. "The others." She pointed vaguely in the direction of Anvil's study.

Chevelle walked past me and from the room without another word, but Ruby jumped aside as he neared the door. I raised a brow.

She leaned out the doorway to peer after him, only looking back to me when he'd cleared the corridor.

I smirked before joining her to go.

"What?" she answered. "I thought he was going to pluck my ears off."

We entered the study and Ruby took her place among the others, purposefully walking wide of Chevelle.

I really should have discussed this with him first.

"Call another gathering," I said. "No pomp, this will be a congress." I glanced at Anvil. "Bring in the clan leaders singly.

And anyone else of note." My eyes traveled down the circle. "Steed, you and Grey flank Ruby all evening. Rhys and Rider, post by the south entrance. All others will be sealed." I didn't look at Chevelle or Anvil when I directed them. "Anvil at my left. Chevelle at the opposite end of the long table. I want you in my line of sight at all times." This brought a few peculiar stares, but I kept on. "Tomorrow."

They had their orders and they knew it was serious. Now came the part I'd been dreading. Chevelle and Anvil would understand. If not my choice, then at least my reasoning. It was why Asher had wanted me. It had been a constant battle to stay on the throne. He had needed a powerful second to rule without challenge.

I would have to do the same. It was my only option.

The others deserved to know my motivations. I would have to make them understand. I opened my mouth to speak, but they all froze. They'd heard something I hadn't... or maybe something I'd ignored. The pat of boots against stone grew louder.

My guard were on their feet. Grey was at the door first. At the sight of him, the watchman yelled, "Rogues, south gate."

I gritted my teeth and ran. I wasn't as fast as the others, but I'd been running these corridors since I was a child.

We burst from the castle as one, and the seven formed up around me as if they'd been doing it for years. The yard was bloody. The rogues had worked fast. There were twenty of them, a ragtag band of thugs with greased hair and spiked armor. I scanned the faces and found Vandrell, son of Stryder.

He was huge, his fists as large as my head, and he was ugly. His jaw was misshapen and scarred from fighting, his cheeks stained with animal blood. War paint. They used it when raiding the villages. His hair was tied back, too high on his head, and the front of it stood in pointy tufts.

He was staring at Ruby.

"Reform," I yelled, and they followed without question. They had seen.

Now Steed and Grey stood before Ruby, Rhys and Rider at her sides. Anvil and Chevelle had stayed in position, but I stepped through them to the front of the line.

The rogues came to rest, waiting for my reaction. They were enjoying their little outing, they wanted to drag it out, revel in their triumph. They were fools. I let my eyes roam the line, falling on each of them. Their leather was worn black, their armor dented from battle. A few wore mail. All carried hammers.

"You raid my castle as if it were a village," I accused.

"You will fall, halfbreed," Vandrell answered. "And the fey whore will decorate my pike." With that, he raised the weapon in the air, hammer still at the ready in the other hand.

"Save the pike," I said levelly to the seven behind me.

Vandrell roared and the twenty rushed forward, joining in the battle cry.

I didn't take time to wonder how many of our people they had killed, to worry whose blood covered their hammers or splattered the yard. It didn't matter now. There was only one way, only one justice. I raised my hand and Vandrell was silenced first. Power shot from my palm and shattered his heart. Fire erupted beside him, lightning burst from behind. There was a flash as two more collapsed, all before I'd focused a second attack. A crunch of bone, the thick wetness exploding flesh.

Twenty men, twenty *warriors* fell on the stone without so much as a weapon being raised by my guard.

I walked forward, among the bodies of the fallen, and reached down for the pike. When I turned, my guard remained motionless in their formation. I moved to Ruby, and placed the pike in her hand.

"Tomorrow," I said, looking over my shoulder to Anvil. "Congress."

I wasn't sure how I'd gotten blood on myself. I couldn't remember being close enough. I scrubbed at it, thinking of the stares I'd received on the way back to my room. Everyone had been watching. It had happened so fast, I wasn't sure how, but they had all found a window to lean out, a doorway to peek around, some way to watch. I hadn't wanted to leave the others to clean up the mess, but I couldn't stay when I'd realized the size of our audience.

I knew they would take care of it. They would honor those of our people who'd been killed before we arrived. They would report to me who had been taken and I would pay tribute to them, show my respect to their families. And Ruby would spike Vandrell's head.

I stopped scrubbing. My skin was raw.

I dressed in clean pants and a loose tunic and returned to my room. There was a shuffle outside, but I didn't go to check who was on duty. I stared out the window, into the empty darkness of night, and then closed my eyes, searching for the wolves. I hadn't felt them since I'd returned from our journey. They must have left while I slept.

I wondered where they were. I wondered if they knew about Junnie. I wondered what I was supposed to do with all this power, why they'd brought Rhys and Rider, whether they'd known about Asher, why the rogues chose today to attack, and who else wanted me dead. I wondered when I'd get some sleep.

Late the next morning, a light knock sounded at my door. I was already awake, but my voice was still hoarse when I answered. "Yes?"

Ruby poked her head in.

"You're knocking now?" I asked.

She pushed the door open and shrugged. "I brought you some bread."

She sat it on the table by the door, whether because she could tell I wasn't interested or because it had only been an excuse to see me, I wasn't sure.

"I stood the pike by the gate," she said. "For our guests."

A flicker of concern that I'd given Ruby too much authority edged out my other worries for a moment, but when I looked up at her, it appeared she'd simply done what she'd thought I wanted. I nodded. "I suppose that's for the best. I'm sure they've all heard by now."

"The others are still hunting down the clan leaders for tonight," she offered.

"So you are my guard."

She nodded. "And Grey." She paused, looked a little guilty, and added, "And Rhys."

"When Chevelle returns, please let him know I'd like to speak with him." I really needed to tell him my plans before the congress.

Ruby rolled her jaw, but kept her lips tight.

"What?"

"I…"

"Ruby," I demanded.

Her face twisted into a grimace. "I don't know," she started, "but I think he's looking for Stryder."

"Alone?"

She lifted a shoulder. "It isn't as if he can't handle it."

And he'd left me here with no fewer than three guards. I swung my legs off the bed to stand. "How long has he been gone?"

"Too long for you to stop him."

"Then that's how it will be," I said. She was burning to ask, but I ignored her. "Let's get dressed, shall we?"

12

SECOND

The rest of the day was a blur. I'd chosen a form-fitting costume, black and leather. A short cape for freedom of movement, clasped at the shoulders with pewter adorned with the crest of my line. I wore a cuff on my left wrist, but my right was bare. Ruby had painted the hawk and intricate runes there, just above the base of my palm. I was outfitted for a special kind of battle, and my opponent awaited.

I stepped forward, leaving the two watchmen at my private entrance to the hall. The room was silent as I took my place before them, Anvil at my left in all his regalia. The walls had been covered with dark silks and standards, all bearing the crest. The room was smaller than the banquet hall, windowless, and I couldn't help but feel closed in with so many in attendance. The torches and candles flared brighter, and I wondered if Ruby could tell what I was feeling. Hard to say. She did have a flair for the dramatic after all. I scanned the room. It appeared they'd been able to locate representatives for most of the clans. My guard was in place, but I couldn't bring myself to look at Chevelle. What I was about to do…

But no, it had to be done. There was no other I would name.

"I have called this congress…" I heard myself droning the words but I could only focus on the crowd. They had already formed opinions of Chevelle; they had heard the rumors. Some of them had even been here when I had publicly denied him as Asher sought to arrange a marriage. And now, what I was going to do would be like denying him again.

Permanently.

A second was backup, there to step in when the lord fell. They could never be in a union, because one who was bound would likely die themselves if they lost that connection. If I chose Chevelle, if I named him my second, it would be like announcing we would never be bound. Otherwise, it would only be for appearances, for he would not live long after my death.

"… and call you to order as I name my second."

As I made it through the lengthy speech, my eyes finally fell on Chevelle, across the long table. It would be as we always stood at these ludicrous functions now, opposite ends, never side by side.

I felt wretched.

"Chevelle Vattier. Born of North Camber, Guard of the Seven, Second to the Lord." I held his eyes, skipping over the part that listed his mother and father, though it was secret to none. I'd already all but slapped him in the face.

Aside from the intake of breath, which might have been Ruby, silence smothered the room. I gave it a heartbeat, two, three. It crossed my mind that I should have prepared my guard further, but I couldn't be sure, even now, what the clans' response would be. They could oppose it, but it would call for their death to question my order so blatantly. They could fight, but they would lose. They might have had a chance, if they had all agreed, prepared before coming, but they hadn't known. And I had the support of at least a few here. I hoped the rest simply accepted it. Far too many had died only the night before. I didn't want to go through it again.

After several more minutes of quiet, I glanced around the room. For the most part, everyone in attendance seemed confused, and eager to get out with their lives. No one wanted to be caught up in bloodshed here, in the castle.

Chevelle stood completely motionless. Expressionless. As if a statue in the costume of a guard.

"I call you forward to bear this token," I announced.

He seemed hesitant to move and I drew in several long breaths through my nose. The token was nearly meaningless to all others. Mine had been the amulet. The same amulet Asher had previously given my mother. I hadn't wanted it, had returned it to her, and she had worn it the day she burned. It was all that had survived the fire, and they'd left it with me when they'd taken me to the village.

Chevelle finally made his way across the room, coming to stand at my right. I turned to him, nodding to his arm as I pulled the thin leather strip from my belt. I had retrieved it from the box of things he'd returned to me, and when he saw it, I knew he recognized it. The slightest twitch at the corner of his mouth was the only indication he might someday forgive me.

My hands were trembling, but there was nothing to be done for it. I tied the strip around his wrist, knotting it over his cuff to complete the ceremony.

I turned back to face the room. "As the High Guard bears witness, so bear the agents of the north. It is decreed this day, until the hour of our death, by none disputed."

"Hear, hear," the Seven chorused.

"Hear, hear," repeated the crowd.

After that, I had quickly dismissed the meeting and exited the hall. Now I sat perched on top of the castle, watching tiny little bands of the leaders of the realm scurry from the grounds. Even from this height, I could spot Rhys and Rider's shocks of silvery white hair in the moonlight. It was cold, it was late, and I couldn't decide if I wanted Chevelle to show, or if I was petrified he'd find me.

He didn't come.

I fell asleep there, waiting for something happen, or hiding from just that. When I woke, it was full dark, the moon covered by vaporous cloud. I'd been dreaming, an odd one featuring Steed and Ruby. They were flying through the air, drunk on the effects of dust, and she was giggling uncontrollably. It might have been funny, seeing Ruby race through the air, red curls flowing, laughing riotously, if I hadn't been witness to the fairy raids as a child.

They would sneak in, hundreds of them, flitting through the castle at incredible speeds. Some of them were nearly too quick to see, except that they never went unnoticed. Chaos and madness were left in their wake. They destroyed, pillaged, ransacked. They set fires, loosed floods, poisoned. They were tiny, sparkling furies, bent on destruction. Asher had nearly declared war, but was finally able to quell the attacks.

I stood, ready to make my way back for warmth and maybe some food, and was thrown forward, almost knocked from my perch. I grabbed a stone pillar and fell into a squat, looking behind me before jumping down to the roof. It might have been a strong gust of wind. If it hadn't giggled.

As soon as I saw the sky was clear, I leapt from the roof, into the window, and ran through the corridors full speed. It hadn't been a dream. That meant they'd been here too long already.

A dull thump and a scrape echoed through the halls from far off. The torches came alive, flames flaring at full heat. A half dozen more steps and I rounded a corner, finding Grey, who was heading for me at what had to be his own top speed. Where were they?

"East wing," he said, answering my thought.

They'd sent Grey because he was the fastest. At the atrium outside of the east wing, Chevelle and Steed joined us. Chevelle's right side was splattered with blood and glitter. Steed looked as if he might be sick.

"Where is Ruby?" I asked, frantic. Steed glanced toward the clamor. "They will take her!" I shouted. It appeared they'd not even considered the danger.

Chevelle nodded, but I could see his concern lay elsewhere.

I stared down Steed and Grey. "Do not leave her side."

Grey was gone before I'd finished speaking, but we were right behind him. We followed the clatter of metal and chirping laughter to the great hall.

It appeared to have exploded. The furniture was in splinters, pieces of wall and ceiling lay in piles of rubble, the stones of which were being lobbed about by several small gray fey. Their feathers were wet, as was about half the room, which was scattered with patches of ice and puddles of water.

The tapestries were set to a slow burn, though no one seemed to think them significant enough to put out. Given that there were at least a dozen other fairies here who could set even the stone ablaze, I could understand the decision. Anvil had taken to electrocuting a couple of water sprites, which the lilac-skinned Flora and Virtue considered uproarious. They floated above the scene, rolling in the air with laughter.

Rider was cornered by a waiflike winter sprite and two frost monsters were hovering above Rhys, trying to get a hand on his staff. The room hummed with the beat of so many wings and stank of sulfur and spring violets.

"I hate fairies." My voice was surprisingly even.

"Hear, hear," Ruby whispered, catching my eye as she stood behind Steed and Grey midway across the hall.

I drew my sword, grateful I'd stayed in my fighting attire from the evening's meeting. I would have to be careful bandying around magic in a room full of fey. They had a bad habit of affecting energy in unusual ways, and I was barely in control of it myself. I sincerely hoped, once again, that Finn and Keaton had a plan to help me channel it.

"Pretty, pretty," a frost monster murmured to Rhys' staff.

"Anvil," I said with as much calm as I could muster. He ceased transmitting the current toward the water sprites and they shuddered, jerked, and dropped to the floor. They were trembling and muttering incoherently, but their audience became bored.

I stepped in before they found another attraction. "Flora, why have you come?"

Twin amethyst jewels gleamed at me, and I had to focus not to get lost there. Her smile was stunning, though I knew she mocked me. The heliotropes had something very near hypnosis if they could catch you. Her lips were thin, a muted pink against the pale lilac of the rest of her. She wore but a scrap of clothing, revealing the tiny feather-like strokes of mauve covering her body.

Her only response was to purr.

I looked at Virtue. She raised a violet brow.

"Why?"

"You will see, lov-el-y," she taunted, dragging her words out. "You. Will. See."

I stepped forward, sword at the ready. Virtue was more of a soft lavender with the markings of a cheetah. I'd always heard her belly faded to white. Looking at her now, I doubted anyone had actually gotten close enough to find out. She wore the full armor of a warrior fey and a smile that promised to devour.

"He comes," whispered a soft voice from behind the walls.

"He comes," repeated the gray-feathered fiends, forgetting their game of stone-throwing to watch the large hole where the window used to be.

We stood motionless, dreading the "he" who was coming.

No sound accompanied his arrival, but as his form appeared in the opening, the sun broke over the horizon, silhouetting the figure of a winged god in the golden light of dawn.

If I hadn't been so angry, I might have rolled my eyes.

13

VEIL

Veil hovered there for a moment, allowing all to glory in the display. Anvil spat, Grey shook his head, and Rhys struggled to keep his staff from the pale, wiry fingers of the frost monsters.

Finally, Veil spread his arms and drifted into the great hall.

"Nearly through with your presentation?" I asked, not bothering to hide the bitterness in my tone.

He smiled as if I'd applauded him. He tilted his head to the side, perusing my attire. He took his time and when his gaze finally came back to meet my glare, I could practically feel the anger radiating off Chevelle from his position behind me.

"You look well, my Freya," Veil purred.

Something similar to a growl escaped my second, who was, at least for the time being, faithfully guarding my back.

"You look ridiculous," I shot back. "And your insects are swarming the castle."

His smile turned sexy and I tried not to notice that he was indeed worthy of the hero status he had among the fey. "They are not like your little birdies, are they?"

I glared at him. At the moment, there wasn't much else I could really do.

Fey had a knack for knowing absolutely everything. They held secrets that were impossible to learn. It didn't do much good to anyone else, because you could never get information from them and any sort of trade ended with you being in worse shape than when you started. But they knew. And Veil had a special talent for it, so I wasn't surprised that he'd hit me with a very personal endearment and a reference to my ability within the first minute of conversation. But there were only two reasons he would be here now: because I knew something he didn't or because he knew something I didn't.

"Why are you here?" I asked, slowly enunciating each word.

He flew closer, stilling his wings as his soft-soled boots touched the floor. "My dear," he said as he stepped nearer, "you are the talk of the realm. Where else would I be?"

I tightened the grip on my sword.

His gaze flowed over me before he turned his palms up and glanced the room. "And your Seven. My, my, what a glorious mob." His eyes met Ruby's and she held his stare defiantly. I glanced at Grey, but he seemed to be controlling himself... unless you counted the murderous glare.

Veil continued to survey the room, pacing a narrow circle in front of me. He was like a preening peacock, displaying his wares. I wanted to look away, but I didn't trust him that much. So, instead, I watched his effort to impress me with as much disgusted indifference as I could manage.

It was difficult, given that he was shirtless and wore low-slung pants. But I hated fairies. He paraded his lean, muscled torso, gorgeous amber wings dappled with a mesmerizing pattern of swirls and circles, somehow reminiscent of eyes. His eyes. Striking amber gems that complemented his bronzed body, set in a handsome face, adorned with a charismatic smile… He was no less than captivating. But I hated fairies.

I realized he'd stopped moving; he was simply standing there with a satisfied smile, watching me take him in. "Are you quite done?" I snapped.

He replied in a low, seductive voice, "May we speak alone?"

"No." I answered too quickly, and nearly flushed before I caught it. Chevelle went still behind me. "Anything you have to say can be spoken in front of my guard."

Veil's eyes were roaming my body again. "I understand you've chosen a second." There were a thousand implications in his statement, chiefly that I would not be getting bound to Chevelle.

A crash sounded in the corridor, followed by a high-pitched, "Oopsie," and a giggle.

"Get on with it, Veil, before I slaughter your minions."

He appeared oblivious to not only my comment, but all of the destruction surrounding us. "An unexpected choice, your blue-eyed guardian."

I stepped forward. "Spit it out or I'll remove your tongue."

He laughed and glanced at Anvil. I *hated* fairies.

"And especially so soon. You seem concerned for your safety," he said, his eyes falling back to mine.

How he knew within a matter of hours not only that I had chosen a second, but why, was a problem. "It seems you are concerned with my affairs as well," I said.

His face became serious, but retained the sexy. "I am very interested."

I leaned back.

Veil leaned forward. "Perhaps we can make an arrangement."

I was momentarily speechless, and not entirely certain what he was offering.

"I can protect you," he murmured.

My mouth dropped open, and then a few choice words emerged.

"You are very appealing when you're angry, beautiful Freya."

I was tempted to hurt him, but I couldn't afford a war. Not yet.

"No?"

"Never."

"Ah, well." He stepped back, resuming his pacing. "So then, a gift."

I felt a sudden, though light, pull on the cord which held my mother's pendant at precisely the same moment Veil winked at me.

"Let me know if you change your mind," he hummed in an remarkably alluring voice.

I glanced down just as his boots lifted from the floor and found the "gift" attached to my necklace. I didn't waste time unlacing it, instead yanking the entire cord free and away from my skin. When I looked up again, the others were watching a few dozen fey disappear from sight.

Unfortunately, that left far too many still within the hall. The pair of gray-feathered fiends looked at me and smiled. I flinched, not only at their promise, but at what appeared to be blood on their prickly little teeth. I secured the necklace behind my belt and readied my sword.

"Leave now and we will remain at peace."

It was a useless warning. All who'd traveled with Veil had only come to unearth trouble, with the possible exception of Flora and Virtue, who followed him everywhere. But they were gone, along with the ones who didn't care to risk death. Then again, I really wanted them to just go.

The winter sprite who had been harassing Rider moved to the center of the room and joined another of its kind. They were very dangerous, despite their frail appearance. They were nearly as tall as Ruby, but incredibly thin and pale. Their hair was long, a silvery gray that fell down in waves and complemented their paper-thin silver and white wings. And they had the ability to create shards of ice that pierced like glass and broke like steel.

"We have come for the girl," the one farthest from me replied.

I knew exactly who she meant, but I didn't dare take my eyes off them to confirm Ruby's safety. I trusted my guard. They would protect her. Please, let them protect her.

"She will not leave here," I pledged.

As if they had been waiting for the challenge, for my denial, the rest of the fey gathered in a very large half-moon behind them. Except for the frost monsters, who still hovered above Rhys yelling, "Mine, mine," for his staff. I wasn't sure they were even aware of the impending battle, let alone Veil's departure. At least they hadn't tried freezing him yet.

I hated fairies.

"Don't do this." I tried again.

The gray fairy on the right raised a slender hand to ready her troops.

In typical fey fashion, a small male broke the charge early, heading straight for Ruby. Steed's sword came up to meet him and sliced though his thin frame from hip to shoulder, crosswise. It was fortunate he'd flown in low. That was rarely the case.

"Idiot," the second gray fairy muttered.

As the first lowered her hand, Anvil took a knee to steady his shot and threw lightning at the water sprites. He'd been battle-trained to fight the fey. I hoped the rest of my guard knew better than to use much magic. Rhys and Rider moved to cover our backs and Chevelle shifted to my left side. The fey split into approximately three lines, hovering high over our heads, hovering just above us, and at ground level.

It was a brilliant tactic. The largest were on foot, coming at us with magic and weapons. While we were busy chopping them down, the airborne line came at us in formation, while the highest fey took turns swooping in to dive-bomb unexpectedly. Swords flashed, dust flew, wings sang. It was complete and utter chaos.

A robust ginger-skinned male with auburn hair and orange-brown wings came at me with a half-sword and I parried, then cut through his chest on the back swing. As he fell, a gorgeous lithe female, who might have passed for an elf if not for the thin cerulean wings, shrieked a battle cry and leapt in a kick at my face. I dodged and spun, knowing better than to grab her, as she turned to face me. Over her shoulder, I could see Rhys, still struggling with dual frost monsters, who now had hold of his staff.

Chevelle had closed ranks behind me, covering the attack. The fairy flung two knives at me, which I dared not dodge for Chevelle's sake, and spun into another kick. I deflected one of the knives with my sword and held the other with the smallest amount of magic I could release, which happened to be far too much and shattered the blade. The distraction caused me to neglect the kick, and it landed directly over my healing rib. By then I was just mad.

I punched her square in the nose and brought the knife from my hip up to plant in her chest. When I moved to return to the line, I saw the strangest thing. Standing in the center of a triangle formed by Grey, Steed, and Rider stood a glorious red-headed fury. True and steady, she swung her whip in circles around the lot of them. There was no particular pattern, up and over, around, back, down, sometimes swirling above them several times before returning to cover the others. Each time a fairy came in for attack, it met with a sword or risked being tangled by whip, which brought the fliers down neatly for a knife to the gut.

It was inspired, as the rest of us were vulnerable to the air strikes. It made me wonder if that was the reason she'd chosen the weapon. And then I inhaled, which made me wonder if Veil had known about my broken rib.

I edged in between Chevelle, who had amassed an impressive pile of fey corpses, and Anvil, who had efficiently removed the threat of water sprites before they'd had a chance to flood the hall. Two large shadow stalkers rushed forward and I raised my blade to strike. I caught one in the side, but they were fast, and the other dodged the blow completely. As I pulled back, Chevelle sliced through the second with deadly accuracy before turning to deflect a jade fairy's blade. I finished off the shadow stalker just as the advance fell.

The handful of fey that remained were airborne, alternately lunging toward Ruby and then feigning back at her strike.

"Bring them down," I commanded, surprised at my own vehemence. "I want this over with."

My guard responded by surrounding Ruby in a large, loose circle. They watched the air as two russet fey dived simultaneously.

Grey struck one with a miniscule amount of energy, causing it to bounce into the flight path of the second. Off guard, the second was caught by Ruby's whip and slung to the ground by an ankle. Steed sliced its throat. Recovered, the first tried to rebound but was speared through the chest by Rider.

One of the remaining watchers screeched and three others flew wide in a sudden attack on me. I blasted them from the air, hoping they'd not have time to feed off my power, and Chevelle leapt over one and slammed into another, who had already been rising. The few that were left had apparently been driven to madness by their defeat, because they were frantically darting around the room, high-pitched bird-like screams and hisses trailing behind.

Steed began to drop stones from the ceiling, which finally brought them low enough to be caught. Spitting venom and cursing, they fought resembling cats, claws and all.

At last, the room was silent. I glanced around, incredulous at the destruction. Pools of water and blood stood on the dismantled stone floor, the furnishings were scattered shards of wood and metal. Bits of wing littered the ground like so much confetti. My gaze caught as it came across the strange pale scraps covering the floor near the back wall where Rhys had stood. It appeared he'd found a way to deal with the frost monsters. I felt a shiver and turned to the others, who also seemed to be in various stages of shock and post-combat unrest.

"Steed, take Ruby to her room. Bar the door."

He snapped out of his stupor quick enough.

"Grey, Rhys, Rider, search the castle. I don't want to find any strays later by accident."

They didn't waste any time either, which left three of us alone.

I turned to Anvil. "How did they get here so fast?"

He shook his head. "It isn't impossible, but they likely discovered your decision on the way."

"So, why were they coming?"

"To celebrate your return?" he offered.

I scoffed.

"It is possible Veil has heard of the attempts."

"I agree." I bit my lip, considering. "See what you can find out."

"Indeed," Anvil said, touching his fist to his chest.

Chevelle and I stared after him, remembering the bloody battle and the proposal by Veil.

"When this is over…" he growled.

"I know," I answered. *War*.

14

PRISONER

For as long as I could remember, even during those times I couldn't remember, I'd had one thought, one obsession: If I could just overcome this one insurmountable obstacle, then things would be bearable.

But my whole life had been a series of those hurdles, and each time I crossed one, there was nothing but another on the other side. A chasm, a mountain, one more impossible challenge. As I stood there with Chevelle, wanting only to right the Council's wrong, to avenge my mother and my kingdom and be done with it, I could see nothing but more problems on the horizon.

I pulled the necklace from my belt and stared at the pendant beside my mother's. It was a long spike, formed by four smaller twisted strands. It was an odd sensation, as two of the strands were cold, the other two warm, but I didn't think it was charmed as I'd feared at first. What had Veil meant by it? There was no question the fey were tricksters, but they were clever as well. This was no simple gift, but had he meant it for a warning, or a promise? He'd seemed sincere in his proposal, though he hadn't given the pendant until I'd declined his offer.

I couldn't blame Veil for the others, for all that had happened, but I couldn't entirely trust him either. Between the lot of them, they'd invaded my home, insulted my second, and attempted to steal my guard. And who knew what the ones we hadn't seen were doing.

I glanced at Chevelle, who seemed to have his anger under rein now. "We should probably help the others."

He moved to place his hand at my lower back as we started for the corridor, but stopped just short of touching me. I pretended not to notice.

The halls were a quiet mess. The staff tended to stay in their rooms during a fairy raid, so the corridors were empty aside from the fabric, beads, broken furnishings, and occasional foodstuffs scattering the floors. We came across a door covered in ivies, another painted with profanities, and a third busted through. Oddly enough, the libraries were intact.

"Wouldn't want to destroy those, they might need to borrow a book," I muttered.

At the end of another hall, right before the entrance to the kitchens, was a large T-wall. I stood staring for a long moment at what appeared to be a portrait of the new lord of the north. Naked. It was plainly a hurried job, but all the important parts were there. I turned to Chevelle, but couldn't decide whether he was trying to conceal a grimace or grin. I took the time to glare at him before moving on, just in case.

Hurried footsteps caught up with me shortly, but they were delayed enough that I knew he'd taken care of the graffiti.

The fey had managed a considerable amount of damage to the castle in the short time they'd been liberated, but no one had been badly injured. The kitchen staff had had it the worst—there were plenty of utensils to clang around and batter with—though I'd not checked the stables. They always had fun in the stables. I kicked a broken crate from my path.

"We've got one," Grey announced from the doorway, and I turned to find him ragged, clothes torn, face scratched.

"A lion?" I asked.

He had no sense of humor after what he'd been through. His answer was flat. "A fairy."

We met him at the door. "Thank you, Grey. Go see Ruby before she tears Steed apart."

They held the tiny female in an unused room, empty of all but a wrought iron chair and two irritated guards. Rhys and Rider weren't scraped and tattered as Grey had been, but they didn't get agitated much so I figured she must have been a difficult one. They had bound her to the chair at the wrists, ankles, elbows, knees, thighs, waist, and chest. The chair had been bound to the stone. I didn't ask what they'd done to the chains to keep her from working free, because I was afraid the answer was a spell.

I walked closer, though I'd learned my lesson from coming too near our last prisoner, and nodded toward the gag. Rider reached in and yanked it free. A stream of curses followed, I assumed picking back up directly where she'd left off when he'd shoved the rags in her mouth in the first place. It was quite impressive, and I let her run with it for a few moments to wear herself down.

"... son of an imp and your mother was an unbonded flaxen *whore!*" she finished.

Rhys had gone pale. Apparently, neither he nor his brother had dealt with many fairies before. Rant ended, she turned her gaze to me and her natural beauty returned, smoothing her face into ethereal magnificence beneath sun-kissed chestnut curls. The light streaming in through the small, slitted windows behind her reminded me that it wasn't even midday. I suddenly felt exhausted.

"Why are you here?" I asked, skipping the introductions.

Her gaze flicked to Rider. "Because this ignorant ram's ass tied me to a chair."

"Indeed." I cleared my throat. "But why were you here, in the castle, before you were tied to a chair?"

She smiled. "Surely you would know, Lord Freya." She added enough sweetness to my name to make it perfectly clear she'd used the endearment as satire.

"Veil is gone. The others are dead."

Only the slightest flicker of emotion flashed, too brief to tell whether it was worry or anger, but long enough to be certain she hadn't meant to be left behind.

"I know you are not a spy, but it is too dangerous to keep you here."

For a fraction of a second, she was relieved to hear of her coming release. And then she realized she'd mistaken my meaning completely. "What will it take?" she asked.

"The truth."

"Each holds his own truth. What will it take?"

"Why are you here?"

"Because I was bored," she answered. "That is my truth."

"And the others? What was their purpose?"

"I cannot know."

"Then you cannot live. I will not waste the lives of my guards watching you, nor risk them for the same." I turned to leave.

"I could guess," she offered nonchalantly as I reached for the door.

"What do you suppose, then?" I asked, turning back to face her.

She shrugged. "Might have been the girl. The grays seemed very interested in bringing her back."

"For whom?"

She shook her head. "I am guessing, remember?"

"You've heard."

"I hear a lot of things, it doesn't make them true."

"And Veil's truth?" I asked. "What is that?"

Her eyes peered into mine. It was more than a little disturbing, but not as disturbing as her statement. "He does want you."

"Why was he here?" I asked, forcing my tone to steady.

She glanced at my neck, seemed confused, and then shrugged it off. I waited. "There was some sort of gift," she said finally.

I nodded. "And what do you know of this offering?"

She shook her head. "Gift. And I know nothing."

"Release her," I said to Rhys and Rider. "She's of no use to us."

It was essentially true, but mostly I wanted her to stir a few things up on her way back to the fey lands so Anvil's contacts might be able to gather the information we needed.

Chevelle followed me to the hall, ready to resolve the disasters left behind by the fey.

"When Anvil returns, we will meet," I said, drained.

When I finally made it to my room, I unlaced my shirt and took a long, deep breath. I was fairly certain the kick I'd taken had set my recovery back a few more days, but it wasn't as painful as it had been the first time, and I was grateful for that. Leaving my boots on, I stretched out on the bed to close my eyes.

The lightest whisper of footsteps outside my door let me know my guard was once again on duty. I sighed.

Lying down intensified the fatigue tenfold, but I didn't sleep. I searched the mountains, reaching for the minds of Finn and Keaton. I wasn't able to find them, so I moved ahead to my next task and located my hawk. He had fled the castle in the raid, but was perched nearby one of the gates. I set him to flight and circled the grounds.

Apparently, the fey had been warned to come in stealth, because nothing outside of the yards was damaged. I could see the staff now, annoyed at the mess, but relieved to be unharmed as they tried to set things to rights. I had a feeling it was going to take them a while. Continuing my inspection, I checked the roofs, crevices, anywhere the fey might be hiding or might have left a snare.

Eventually, I came to the stables, saving my most dreaded chore for last. I really didn't want to see what they'd done there this time. The hawk alighted on a post outside the stable and I was surprised to see Steed walking a mare into the yard. He must have come straight to check on his stock as soon as Grey had relieved him of his charge. I hopped to a nearer post.

The poor beast was covered in a shimmering violet dust and Steed stood beside her, humming while he gently brushed it away. I bounced to the post closest to them, and saw the ground was littered with various shades of the stuff. He must have brought each one out and swept them clean by hand. The way he looked, I was curious if he'd done this for the animals or himself. Surely, he could have been done much quicker by other means. His hum to calm them—the way Ruby had hummed me to sleep so many times before my recovery—broke into song then, and the corner of my mouth drew up.

Steed was so engrossed in his work, he had only glanced at the bird when it landed near him. It wouldn't have seemed unusual, after all, because it lived in the castle. But as I watched him, he began to glance more frequently at the hawk. Apparently it didn't normally stalk him.

The mare purred and Steed answered in a low tone. "Yes, darling." She rolled a shudder down her back, shaking out more dust. "There's a girl," he murmured.

I cocked the head of my host sideways just as Steed flicked another glance at it. His eyes narrowed infinitesimally. I wasn't certain it was his audience that had him unnerved, but it sure seemed that way. I thought I'd check. As he moved to work the dust from the mane of the mare, rubbing between her ears, he glanced over again. I raised one clawed foot from the post and held it forward in salute.

It was definitely the bird. His face twisted into an unease I'd never before seen on him. Singing stopped, he stared straight ahead, over the mare's back.

I sprang to the mare's rump, landing lightly about a foot from his face. He jumped.

I felt myself chuckle back in my bed and then was startled out of the hawk by a familiar voice.

"Freya."

I didn't know why I felt guilty, but I bolted upright, and then winced at the pain in my side from the sudden move. Chevelle handed me a cup, and I took it without thinking. It was warm against my hand and smelled wonderful. One sip and I was choking and spitting uncontrollably.

"Ruby prepared a blend for your rib."

I wheezed.

"She mentioned it might be strong."

I looked up at him, completely unable to form a response.

He smiled. "Rest, Freya."

~

It must have worked, because the next thing I knew, Ruby was waking me for our meeting. She seemed well, considering the fey had apparently placed a bounty on her. I took a breath before questioning her, realized it didn't hurt, and took several long, deep lungfuls of air.

"Ruby, what did you give me?"

She shrugged. "Tea. Now, come on." She threw clothes at me, impatiently moving about the room while I put myself in order.

"You're keyed up," I mentioned as I walked toward the door.

"Maybe I just don't like waiting," she snapped. She walked two paces in front of me all the way to the study, clearly not wanting to discuss whatever had her edgy. It definitely wasn't fear, though.

When we entered, she pointedly did not look at Grey, which of course caused me to. He was staring at her with an intensity that would have caught a normal woman on fire. Ruby, however, had been born of fire.

I shook my head. This was just what we needed.

All eyes fell on me as I stepped to the head of the table. I threw the pendant down, the twisted strands landing with a clanging thump on the wood surface.

"Ice, silver, blood, and bone. Our gift."

15

GIFT

They stared at the pendant, the spike formed from four intertwined strands. There was no question in my mind the ice and silver were related to my attacks, especially since Veil had mentioned my safety. How they were related was another matter entirely. They were cold to the touch, while the blood and bone were warm. A gift, our prisoner had insisted. Leave it to the fey to offer a puzzle instead of a clear message.

"It's the same," Ruby said, wide-eyed. She hadn't had a chance to examine the pendant yet, to see the thin thread of ice, frozen solid even now.

"I suspected as much." I glanced at Chevelle. "And the silver?"

"It appears so," he answered, none too pleased with the revelation.

"The question remains, is this admission of their involvement, a threat of further attacks? Or is this truly a gift, answer to our search?"

Rider leaned forward. "Why would they admit their own involvement? Why not just fight with full force if that was what they wanted?"

"For that matter, why would they help you by handing you the enemy?" Ruby asked.

Chevelle tensed beside me; both questions could be answered by Veil's interest in me.

"I don't understand," Rhys said, "why they would risk it at all."

I waved a hand dismissively. "They've been doing it for ages, never mind that half of them are killed. They don't consider it risk, just a good night out."

"There's something else," Grey said. We all took notice of his tone. "They didn't offer a trade." It was obvious what he meant. They had wanted Ruby.

The room was silent for a long moment before Anvil finally spoke up. "It means nothing. Veil would not soil his hands so publicly in such an arrangement. By coming, he has already placed himself on unstable ground."

"About that," I interjected. "This was the largest force I've seen for a very long time. There were no fire fairies."

Anvil nodded. "Hard to say at this point, but I am hoping they support your choice." He paused, considering. "That's not to say they would not welcome her return, unwilling as it were."

Steed changed the subject. "As for the pendant, is the blood meant for death, or lineage?"

"That, as well as the bone, can be interpreted in many ways," Anvil answered. "The fey are not easy to read. And they like it so."

Rhys was disgusted. "Then this token is worthless."

I shook my head. "No. Even if we don't understand their motives, even if we never decipher their clues, it tells us one thing for certain. The two attacks were connected and the fey know how."

"If this is a threat"—Steed shifted uncomfortably—"then no response is an act of battle in itself."

Ruby nodded. "And Veil's going to work up a good lather over your refusal."

"And then they'll be back." Steed added. "In force."

"No." Chevelle's voice was cutting. I wasn't positive he'd meant to speak at all.

I sighed, needing to explain to the others but not wanting to voice the problem. But I had to. The fey loved a good war and if they could manage it, they'd be back soon enough. The group we'd dealt with had been nothing, merely along for the ride, toying with us over Ruby. A true raid would have left us more damage than a few scrapes and bruises.

"Some fey have the ability to manipulate the magic of others. A strike against them can be turned, distorted…" I shook my head. "Let's just say it's ugly. The problem is, with my magic in such a volatile state, I would be risking not only myself, but the release of these powers to the fey."

"To Veil," Chevelle said.

There was a collective silence while everyone in the room imagined the flying amber god with the combined energy of himself, myself, and all that Asher had amassed.

Ruby had gone pale. I decided to throw her a bone. "Finn and Keaton may be able to assist with this. They have brought us Rhys and Rider for a reason, and I believe their connection plays a part. When the wolves return, we may have one less problem to worry about."

Ruby immediately lost all concern for our crisis. "The legends are true? The wolves are the ancients?" She stared at me a moment before her scarlet curls whipped around to find Rhys and Rider, both of whom smirked. I would have to remember to thank them for that later.

The meeting ended with nothing at all resolved. Anvil hadn't been able to discover anything useful in his first attempts, but he intended to try again now that we had released our captive fairy back into the wild. Grey and Steed were planning a trip to Camber under the guise of guard duties to see if they could learn anything useful. Ruby had flatly refused their offer to go along, which I attributed to the sparks that were flying between her and Grey and to the possibility of her missing Finn and Keaton's return.

She followed Rhys and Rider from the room, but they were tight-lipped. They seemed to be thoroughly enjoying themselves and I wondered what she'd done to them to merit the torment.

Chevelle and I were all that remained in the study. He stood staring at the pendant on the table.

I watched him. "You think Veil made the offer because he knows of my uncooperative powers."

Chevelle let out a breath before raising his gaze. The emotion in it was crippling. "No. He has always wanted you." His eyes fell to my lips and my throat went dry.

"You think we should trust him?" I rasped.

A sardonic smile answered my disbelief. "I think he wants you safe." Chevelle's hand slid across the table, moving closer. "For him."

I purposefully directed my gaze to the pendant. "Then it's a warning. But a warning against a fey campaign, or someone else?" The twisted strands of silver and ice caught the flicker of the torchlight, shimmering like the ornament of a fairy, not an elvin lord. "If it is someone else, we need to decipher it. And if it is the fey, then there is no way to stop them from coming for me." I contemplated the devious, underhanded war tactics of the fey, thought through what would happen, and then remembered what Chevelle had said. "And he wouldn't let them have me, would he? If they come, he can't stop them. But he won't... *can't* allow them to have my power. He would take me."

I felt the change in Chevelle beside me, but I dared not look up. There would be nothing I could do to fight Veil without risking the release of my power, but I had no doubt of Chevelle's intent.

"I will find control," I promised. "And we will solve the pendant."

Regardless of who was trying to kill me, I still had a kingdom to run. So as I worked to catch up and set right all that had gone undone in my absence and awry since my return, I puzzled out the clues. I knew one thing for certain now: the attackers were Asher's offspring. The boy's coloring was likely due to a mixed birth. And the fact that the fey were involved made me wonder if the ice attacks were not from a half-fey child. Ruby, after all, had turned out strong and dangerous. Fortunately, she was on my side.

I had mentally crossed the rogues off the list, as the massacre in the yard would have never come to be if they had control of anyone in line for the throne. They were brutal, but they had enough sense to use a tool like that in the most effective way: they would have gathered a following. If it was the fey who had control over an heir, then they were either just playing with me until they could place him or her, or they had more than one and they were trying to thin out the stock, neither of which were highly likely. Still, I couldn't stop the shiver that ran through me at the thought of a fey-influenced lord on the northern throne. But even if they didn't have a child or children, then they knew who did, and at the very least were tracking the situation. I had the strands of silver and ice to prove that.

So that left two options that I could think of: Asher and Junnie. Asher had not been gone long. He could have spent years training and molding his children, he could have told each they were his rightful heir, and they could be coming for me because I stood in his place. The attacks had not come together. The silver boy had been alone, and he had called me the pretender. But if Asher had done this, if he was the cause, then there was nothing to be done but wait for the others to decide it was time. There was no way to find them, to flush them out.

There was a way to find Junnie, however. And Junnie was, right now, raising a child of Asher's. A half-human child whose mind she could possess. Junnie had been with me in the village, so she couldn't have raised the other children. But she could have taken them when Asher was on the run. They hadn't been with her when we had found her, but she had a following by all accounts, and there could be someone supporting her. Someone who wanted the new Council, who wanted control of the entire realm. Maybe an army of someones. Maybe a new Council had already formed. I shook my head, silently praying once more that it wasn't Junnie.

I didn't even consider Grand Council on my list, even though they too had wanted reign over all. Not because their key players had been removed and they were at this moment regrouping, not because they wouldn't do it if they could. I didn't consider them because in a matter of days, there would be no more Council.

I would finally avenge the wrong done my mother. I would repay the debt owed my people. In a matter of days, there would be one less barrier before me, one less cross to bear. Days.

"Frey?"

"Oh, sorry, Ruby. Please continue."

She glanced at the scrolls, a large pile of messages from across the realm, and I could tell she was calculating how much longer it would take to finish.

"It comes with the uniform, Ruby. The guard has never claimed one who was merely a fighter. If you want to choose the dead, you have to manage the living. It keeps us from turning murderous."

She cocked a brow at me, knowing full well Asher's guard had been more deadly than productive. But they had all been given other chores. Not decent, moral duties, I thought, remembering Riven and his charge, but duties nonetheless.

Ruby picked up another scroll. "Alianna Denae of Camber is with child. The child's father, Klave, was killed by the rogues outside our gates. She is grieving badly and it is feared she'll not make it to full term."

Manage the living. "Send her an invitation to the castle. Note that she is to come when the child is well and they will be safe to travel. Maybe we can give her something to look forward to."

Ruby nodded, pleased that she might yet have something enjoyable to oversee.

"If she takes a turn for the worse," I added in a hushed tone, "assure her the child will have a place here."

Ruby's eyes held mine for one long moment before returning to the scrolls. She had been an orphan, abandoned by all but her half-brother Steed. In this single task, I had given her reason enough to serve all others. By this lone thing, she understood. She was of the guard.

Her shoulders straight, she relayed the next message.

16

THREAT

I sat on the edge of my bed, twirling the fey spike in my hand. Ice, silver, blood, and bone. A gift. The words had begun to circle, as twisted in my mind as the strands that formed the pendant. I tried to force them away, to see the puzzle from another angle, but they were only replaced with other chants. The dream of my mother, her warning that others would come. And the other warning, words not of a vision, but a living nightmare. *Fellon Strago Dreg.*

I dropped the pendant on the side table and lay back to focus on something that was actually productive. I found my hawk and scanned the grounds, covering the mountain as best I could. No sentry out of place, no strangers with light hair, no ice-wielding half-breeds or winged shimmering fey army. I checked for smaller inconsistencies, anything that would indicate a problem. But I found nothing, and after a long while, the search became more of an easy glide and I felt my body back in the bed relaxing with the task.

Chore accomplished, I thought I might be able to finally get some sleep. But just before I pulled from the hawk's mind, I spotted

Steed in the yard. I drifted down, landing on the parapet to watch him prepare for the trip to Camber. His humming stopped the moment my talons touched stone. I smiled, though he would never see it. Wings stretched, I glided past him, not missing the way his shoulders tensed as the bird passed behind his back. He latched the pack tight against his horse, resolutely not looking my way. I swung around to settle on a post opposite him. Stone-faced, he cinched Grey's pack to the second horse.

I waited him out, certain he couldn't keep his gaze from finding mine for long. When he at last broke, I held utterly still. And winked. His expression was priceless. With a much-needed laugh, I returned to myself and kicked off my boots to finally get some rest.

It was the last I'd have, because when I woke by the light of dawn, there was someone in my room.

Instinct tore at me to move, but I was trapped. Some unseen force had turned my limbs to lead and I could do nothing but stare up into the face of a fey idol.

Veil held himself above me, bare torso inches from mine, fisted hands on either side of my immobile shoulders. I opened my mouth to curse, but my chest had the same heaviness as the rest of me and my lungs seemed empty of air.

"You should have heeded my warning," he whispered so quietly I had to strain to hear. "You have disregarded the gift in your eagerness for vengeance."

I stared up at him, contemplating whether to hear him out or risk using magic. My chest rose and fell unbearably slow beneath him. He glanced down.

Suddenly, as if he realized too late what my reaction to such a gesture would be, he was closer, peering into my eyes as he

153

whispered, "No. Do not tempt me by using your power." He was so near I could see his pulse hammering, but I didn't know whether it was fear or excitement. Sometimes with the fey they were one and the same.

He shook his head. "Revenge tastes sweeter with time, my Freya." His gaze roamed my face, the dark strands of hair across my pillow, the bare flesh of my neck.

I narrowed my eyes at him, and felt the thickness in my throat giving. It wouldn't be long before I was free of the dust. A few more minutes and I would strangle him. Veil could see the change in me and his mouth turned down in what I would have called a grimace on a less attractive man. His wings flicked once in frustration.

He knew he was out of time. I wondered who stood guard behind my closed door, unable to hear his words, no louder than a breath.

Veil's warm eyes met mine, the color of honeyed tea in the morning light. But no, darker this near… more like maple sap over stone. I mentally shook myself, trying to work through the drug. It wasn't the same as Ruby's blend, but it wasn't right, either. He waited for me to focus on him again. He wanted my attention.

"If you do this," he warned, "you will leave me no choice."

As far as warnings went, this one was pretty clear. I wondered briefly why he'd taken such an un-fey-like action. And then I wondered how he could possibly smell so good. And then I remembered I hated fairies and wondered if I could drive the spiked pendant on the table through his side without risking my magic. The last thought made me smile, which clued both of us in on the fact that I'd regained muscle control.

We reacted at the same time, my head snapping forward to slam into his chin just as he moved back and off the bed. I flipped myself up to land beside the bed, but I wasn't fully recovered and my legs crumpled beneath me. From nowhere, Veil grabbed my upper arm to steady me. My right fist swung across to strike him in the side. The scuffle had lasted only a fraction of a second, but it was enough. Rhys burst through the door and Veil was gone.

"Find Ruby!" I yelled, my voice weak but anger propelling the command with sufficient force Rhys didn't stop to question it.

I stared down, panting, struggling to manage the effects of dust and adrenaline. It seemed like only seconds later when Chevelle showed up, but it must have been longer, because my breathing was steady and I could feel the tingle of my legs and the cold of the stone floor where I sat.

He surveyed the room, searching for any lingering threats, and I knew the instant his gaze found the glitter on the bed.

My head fell into my hands, a very unlordly gesture, and my shoulders shook with silent, frustrated hysteria.

Chevelle was staring down at me. "What did he want?"

"To warn me." I took a deep breath before attempting to stand. "The fey don't want us to take out Council."

"Since when do the fey care about elvin politics?"

I shrugged. "I don't know, but if they know we're coming, then Council does."

"It doesn't matter," Chevelle said. He stepped closer. "Tell me what he said."

I took another deep breath.

He waited.

"'If you do this'"—I sighed—"'you leave me no choice.'"

Chevelle's fist slammed into the bed post, splintering the wood to pieces.

"It has to mean they have always cared about our affairs," I said. "But the power was shared before, split between the north and the villages."

He didn't respond, staring blankly across the room, through the empty space where the bedpost had been.

"So if we remove the remaining leaders of Council," I continued, "then I alone control the realm."

Chevelle turned his gaze to me.

"And if I control the realm"—I paused to swallow, throat still thick from dust—"then they will call war. And Veil will take me. If I don't find a way to manage this power, then I can't fight him."

I could see the anger building through Chevelle's entire body, but I couldn't prevent myself from finishing.

"I will avenge my mother. I will right the wrong done to all of the north. The fey will not cow me into submission. We will leave at dawn as planned."

It felt a little like a speech and I should have been ashamed for making it. Chevelle knew exactly what Council had done to the north. He knew every single person who'd been slaughtered in the massacre and he knew how it had affected the ones who lived. He didn't need to be lectured on honor or principle.

His shoulders rose very slowly in an effort to remain steady with each breath. "Vengeance can wait."

His words tasted far too much like Veil's warning and the fury of his attack, as I lay helpless in my own bed, went through me. "No," I hissed. "I will not be controlled."

I had meant by the fey. I had meant by Asher. But it hadn't come across as such.

"Curse you, Frey." Chevelle's voice was pure rage and I almost stepped back from him. As if he sensed it, he stepped forward, daring me.

We stood inches apart, both of us furious, both struggling to retain control, when suddenly Ruby was beside us, frantic.

"Are you hurt? What happened? What did Veil do to you?"

I shook myself, mind catching up with events. I'd heard a light slapping sound when she'd come in and stared down at our bare feet on the stone floor.

"Ruby," I said, "you have webbed toes."

She shoved me back into a chair with unnecessary force. "She's been dusted," she announced with more than a little irritation, and I laughed. It might have been dust or madness, but it didn't much matter.

At the exchange, Chevelle seemed to deflate a bit. And then, realizing he had work to do, he walked from the room, leaving me with Rhys and Ruby. That only left Rider to help him search the grounds, so I leaned back in the chair as Ruby fluttered about me making what I hoped was a remedy, and found my hawk. I doubted we'd see anything. Veil had likely come alone, and he had a talent for hiding.

It was no accident he'd come when the others were gone. He'd taken his best chance, and he'd done it. He'd beaten my guard, bested all of us by sneaking into my bedchamber.

The hawk dove through the castle window and rose above the yard, searching. I had an irrational thought that it hated fairies too and wished the dust would let go already.

Ruby was mumbling as she worked, complaining about the

fey and their gifts, and I came back, opening my eyes to stare at her. Her gaze was narrowed on the pendant atop the side table. The gift.

"That's it," I said.

She jerked, curls bouncing, and then shrugged my outburst off as an effect of the dust.

"No," I defended. "The gift. She kept saying 'gift,' not offering. It isn't about the pendant. It's about the boy. The silver boy."

Ruby stared blankly at me while she decided whether I was babbling or if she should be attempting to decipher my words.

I pointed to the pendant. "Four strands. The fey call them 'gifts', not talents or abilities. Silver and ice. That leaves two more. Blood and bone. He's got four children remaining." I shook my head. "No, three now. We killed the boy."

Understanding washed over her. Her mouth came open, brows raised, then her face fell. She was speechless.

"Ruby," I snapped, "give me that tea and go figure out what the devil blood and bone means."

She barked a laugh. "It isn't tea." She shrugged at the question in my expression. "Veil doesn't work that way. It's more of a... skin rinse."

I opened my mouth to reply just as Ruby closed one eye in a wince and turned her cheek to me. Warm, cloudy liquid splashed into my face. Instantly, the effects of the drug cleared, but were replaced with utter shock at her action. She dropped the cup, putting both hands up in surrender as she backed from the room.

"It had to be done," she promised.

I was still staring at the open door when Rhys finally laughed.

17

BREAKING

Finn and Keaton had still not returned. Ruby and I sat in the study with Rhys and Rider poring over fey scrolls and books. I'd been able to find a few notes hidden in Asher's private study, but it didn't look as if we were going to find anything useful. Anvil was due back by evening, as were Steed and Grey, so we held a sliver of hope they would be able to offer some help. I hadn't seen Chevelle all day.

Ruby slammed a book shut in frustration. "Even if we find the answer, even if we know this kid's 'gift,' it still doesn't solve the problem."

We all stopped working to give her our full attention, though I had a feeling we were just looking for a break.

"If we don't know who's pushing them to attack Frey, then we don't know how to find them. If we find one, or even two, we still have to find the others. We still have to discover who's plotting against us."

I had to fight a smile at her use of "us."

Rider held up a finger. "I believe it is a mistake to consider them children. I understand Asher may have been fostering this

159

strategy before even Francine or Eliza were born. Simply because the one who created silver was a boy does not mean we should expect the same of the others."

Rhys nodded. "If I were the influencer of these 'heirs,' I would send the weakest first."

Ruby's eyes went wide. Apparently, she'd underestimated the cunning of the Strong brothers.

"You are right, though." Rider twirled a quill in his hand as he thought. "We do need to find the source."

"I feel like we're beating our heads against the same rock," I complained.

"At least we know it isn't the fey," Ruby said with mock cheer.

No, I thought, they wanted to either keep us balanced or own us all. With a sigh, I returned to the passage I'd been reading on rare fey talents.

The fey liked to keep records of other people, but preferred no written history of themselves. I had always assumed that was why so many fey tales were spoken. And surely they considered it a bonus, the embellishments that came along with stories passed by word of mouth. But I supposed it was safer that way as well. How much had Ruby learned from her mother's diary...

As I scanned the pages, I recalled the fey visits when I'd been bound in the village. They'd caused no ruckus among the light elves, but they'd only been allowed to come one at a time, occasionally in pairs, to study the libraries. And, if I really thought about it, I had no idea whether they'd caused trouble in the village. For all I knew, they'd been the ones messing with the Council documents, not Fannie. Fannie, who had burned that village to the ground.

I didn't dream much of Fannie since regaining myself. The nightmares I had now were those of my mother. But now the flames were real, memory instead of vision, and they were so much more disturbing with added details like the taste of smoke and scent of blood. Every night, the screams of the slaughter tore through me, the sound of my mother's crazed laughter as they burned her, the pain ripping my own chest as I stood helpless, as I was dragged away. The icy water pulling me under, stealing my breath.

Chevelle had held me back, the only thing that had saved me that day. He'd pulled me into the water and I had wanted to scream. Liquid filled my lungs, choking me, and I might have wanted it, wanted to be swallowed by that darkness. Except for the fire of vengeance that boiled in my blood.

Ruby had been reading through one of the books from Asher's private study and she went still as she flipped a page. I glanced up at her.

"Frey," she started, but then didn't continue when she saw my face. She wordlessly slid the open book to me.

On the yellowed pages lay a tiny scrap of paper with three words. A ribbon of blue silk was attached to the corner.

I stared at it for a long moment before sliding the silk between my fingers. Nothing on the pages of the book was relevant to the message. Someone must have intercepted the note and simply tucked it away as if it hadn't mattered.

"What does it mean?" Ruby whispered.

I glanced at the table, covered in documents and ancient tomes. "Nothing." I shook my head, coming out of the stupor. "Nothing, Ruby, let's take a break." The light through the windows said it was late afternoon. "We've missed lunch, I'm sure we could all do with something to eat."

I spared one last look at the note before sliding it into my pocket. *Fellon Strago Dreg.* It was like the words were following me. Warning me.

By evening, I'd done all I could to prepare for our departure. Anvil had returned, but he hadn't been able to find anything useful in regard to either the fey plans or the attacks. When I'd told him about Veil's visit, he'd been so angry the hair on my head tingled with electricity before he left me to "go over some final details with the patrols." The sky had lit two shades brighter not long after that.

Steed and Grey had also returned, convinced that no one from here to Camber had seen anything out of the ordinary. We went over the final details for the morning and when Steed and Ruby got into a heated argument about some traps she'd left set in her Camber house, Grey took the opportunity to discuss our purpose.

"They are all still mourning," he said. "The shock of your return, the stir over your recent actions, those have only been a distraction." He absently ran a hand over his jaw. "They need this as desperately as you. We have all lost so much."

I glanced at Steed, whose own mother had been killed in the massacre. It had driven his father so mad, he'd fallen under the thrall of a fire fairy.

Grey sighed. "You are doing right, Frey. And when it's done, they will follow you."

I bit my cheek to stop myself from pointing out it would do no good if one of Asher's progeny found me.

"Thank you, Grey." I squeezed his arm, grateful for his words, and knew Chevelle had not chosen him merely for his connection with Ruby.

"Have it your way, then," Steed seethed as he strode from the room with less than his usual cool.

"I will," Ruby yelled at his back.

When she realized Grey and I were staring at her, she threw her hands up in disgust. "I don't know what's with him lately." She shook her head as she glanced back at the empty doorway. "He's so jumpy, always looking over his shoulder, you'd swear someone was stalking him or something."

A choked cough escaped me, but neither seemed to know why. I simply kept watching Ruby.

Grey tilted his head. "You did leave traps for him, Ruby."

She let out a disgusted sound. "Not for *him*." Her hands moved to her hips. "Besides, he should have known I would have set them."

Grey shrugged. "Well, he found them regardless."

The corner of her mouth raised in a snarl and I was suddenly laughing. Grey turned to stare at me and I shook my head. "I think I need some sleep."

I excused myself and walked the corridor at an easy pace while I considered the coming event. We had given Council time to regroup. It would be a fair fight. I had confidence in my guard, but I couldn't bear the idea of losing any of them. The thought crossed my mind that I could leave, spend my years running with the wolves, but I couldn't even finish it. I wouldn't leave. Not my guard, and not the north. Grey was right, they needed this as much as I. I would never really rest until I'd quenched the flames of my nightmares.

I hadn't been back to my perch since the fey had nearly knocked me from the roof, so I found myself standing in the throne room, staring across the empty space. It had been an ugly childhood, Chevelle the only bright spot. Asher had done all that he could to take that from me, to force me into something I'd never wanted, to secure my place as his second. And here I stood, alone on the throne and separated from Chevelle. Even in death, he'd succeeded.

I took a deep breath as I sat, fingers curling into the ornate carvings on the arms of the chair. My eyes fell closed and I found my hawk to take flight, gliding over the mountain one last time before morning. Darkness had begun to fall and torches lit the grounds like fireflies in a southern meadow. Nightfall brought the revelers out in the towns and rogue camps, but here the sentries were still on duty.

The circles became smaller as I scanned the castle, then finally dropped through a window and down the east wing. I opened my eyes as we came to the corridor outside the throne room and watched the hawk fly in under its own authority to land on the stand beside me.

I smiled at the sizeable bird and it cocked its head with a quick twist.

"Someday, I will name you," I said, gently stroking the feathers along the back of its neck. It shuffled closer, talons claiming the soft wood of the perch. We sat so for a long while, time uncounted as we relaxed together, I as unthinking as the bird.

Finally, it stretched its wings before bringing them back together, shaking as it settled into a solid form, neck disappearing into the mass of feathers, eyes winking shut. "I agree," I murmured, knowing I needed sleep even though the time here had been more restful than any night of the past weeks. I stepped down from the chair, aware once again that it was a throne, and headed to my room.

I walked in the door, tossed my scabbard and sword on a side table, and kicked off my boots. When I rose back to standing, I found Chevelle across from me against the far wall. For a fraction of a second, my heart quit. When it started back up again, I knew I was flushed.

Embarrassment at being caught off guard and frightened made me irritated. "What are you doing?"

His face didn't change, though I knew what he was thinking. Not a day ago, I'd been confronted with a fey idol here. "I will be placing protections on the room."

The anger was genuine now. "What?"

Chevelle remained as he was, but I could see now his posture was set for a fight. "It is the only way—"

My glare cut him off. "You will not cast on or near me."

"I will protect your room," he answered levelly.

"Then put a guard outside."

"A guard outside does no good. He's proven that."

"No spells," I repeated.

"You'll not sleep unprotected."

"Then I'll not sleep alone," I shot back.

I had answered without thinking, but once the words were out, they hung between us, taking on a new meaning. And the longer it hovered there, the stronger it became. He stared at me, gaze unflinching, as I stood motionless, afraid to even breathe.

I knew we shouldn't. There was good reason not to. I was sure of it, even if I'd forgotten exactly what that reason was. A flash of memory, the taste of him, his bare skin beneath my hands, the unbearable feeling of being so near him and still wanting him closer. I forced myself to stop but the hunger in his eyes intensified, as if he knew what I was thinking. He was beginning to look as if he might lose control. I swallowed hard, trying to find a way out, certain I needed to.

It wasn't clear to me, what caused him to break, but he was suddenly moving, and the room seemed to shudder with magic. Power slammed into me the instant before he reached me and I almost managed a word. But when he finally touched me, when his hands came around me, his lips crushed mine, even the notion of speaking was gone.

18

FIRST LIGHT

Hours later, I couldn't say I regretted it. My head lay on his chest as his hand slid slowly up the skin of my arm and across my shoulder. He gently drew my hair away to bare my neck, and then his fingers retraced the line.

"Do you feel any different?" I asked.

His chest rumbled beneath my cheek with a sort of chuckle and I turned to examine his face. He stared at me for a long moment, finally understanding. "You don't know, do you?"

"What?"

Eyes never leaving mine, he let out a slow breath. "We have always been bound, Freya."

I stared at him, unable to process his words.

The corner of his mouth turned up in a gentle, sympathetic smile. The kind you gave a small child when they couldn't possibly understand something larger than their world. But it wasn't offensive. It was beautiful, filled with affection.

"The bond," he explained. "We created it without intent, very long ago."

I was pretty sure my expression fell somewhere between

shock and confusion.

His fingers continued to trail the line of my back. "I think it is usually created while coupling"—he smiled a slow, sexy smile then, remembering, and he tilted his head up to place a kiss on my forehead—"because that is when two are the closest. Their magic, their bodies, their… love." Here I was kissed again, more passionately, and I had to focus hard on what he was saying.

I sat up, which did nothing to discourage him.

"But that can't be right," I said numbly, searching for an argument.

His gaze drifted up to meet mine. The hand that had been tracing lazy circles on my skin stilled.

"The elders," I explained, "they all said it would change us, keep us from being true to anything but ourselves. We would hold our union above all others."

He raised my hand for a kiss. "Do you mean abandoning the throne to run away with me?" he asked, as if he were inquiring whether I'd like a glass of wine. He leaned forward and kissed my forearm. "Or waiting for you when you were trapped… searching for a way to release you… risking all for your return?" His lips trailed farther up my arm, pausing only as he glanced at me once more. "Keeping me close to you, all the while knowing it could cost you your life?"

We were already bound.

For as long as I could remember, I had always wanted him.

He was tied to me.

We were bound.

The idea was overwhelming, but suddenly I couldn't spare it another thought, because his lips had reached my own and I was, once again, lost to the outside world.

Time was non-existent until the shuffle of boots in the corridor pulled me from my contented trance. I sat up suddenly, recalling our plan. "What time is it?"

Chevelle dragged me back against him, tilting his head to place slow kisses on my neck.

It almost worked.

A noise farther down the corridor reminded me that we were late. I pressed back, far enough to kiss him thoroughly, and then free of the bed. His face fell. I smiled.

I was dressed well before he was, securing my scabbard as he laced his shirt. He was in no hurry, but I knew he wouldn't ask me to postpone again. Not after our argument, and not after last night. We would see vengeance. This, at least, would be done.

He sat to fasten his boots and I watched him as I thought again of his promise. *We have always been bound.* My mind had been fighting for some way to dispute the idea, but could only come up with evidence to corroborate it.

Something had always called me to Chevelle. I knew, but I'd simply never understood. How could I? How could anyone?

He raised his head and suddenly I was staring into depthless sapphire. My stomach tightened and I hurriedly turned to open the door. A hand on my shoulder stopped me, and he pulled my hair to the side to place one last kiss on my neck. Wordlessly, we walked from the room, Chevelle settling his leather breastplate as we went.

We found the others in the study, light spilling through the windows making it obvious it wasn't exactly dawn. *Close enough*, I thought, glancing around to be certain everyone was accounted for.

"Steed is readying the horses," Ruby supplied.

I nodded. How she, or any of the others for that matter, had managed not to comment or at least betray some emotion about Chevelle and I was beyond me.

"We are set to go," Anvil agreed.

I supposed that was how they'd managed, knowing what we were about to set out to do. "Then let us go," I said. "For the North."

A harmony of agreement met my oath and we made our way to the yard as one, a small army by all outward appearances. Ruby's curls were smoothed back, a braid from each temple meeting at the base of her neck to form a knot. She had forgone the silver; she and each of the guard had donned black uniforms, insignias marking the shoulder clasps of their dark cloaks. Only the shine of Rhys and Rider's hair stood out among us.

As we walked from the castle, my eyes met Steed's where he waited with the horses. I'd barely had time to process his expression before the sentry called out.

All eyes fell on Edan as he sprinted across the yard. "The fey are attacking Camber, as many as seventy, no structure"—he paused to take a breath as he reached us—"just rioting."

We stood in shocked silence for one moment before the lot of us swung into motion. Chevelle clapped the sentry on the shoulder before he mounted and without another word, eight horses were running through the gates. Steed took the lead, setting a fierce pace and keeping to the path.

I couldn't believe I'd neglected to sweep the skies this morning, knowing that the fey were aware of our plans. I fell in behind Grey and dropped quickly to the horse's mind, urging him to keep pace before finding the hawk. It was perched on a castle wall, tearing meat from a rodent beneath its claw, and I had to force it to flight.

I had intended to make a broad sweep of Camber, but when it took wing, everything fell apart. I froze at what I'd seen, and then heard the clatter of rocks the instant before I opened my own eyes to find Chevelle and Rider had been forced from the path, nearly tumbling into my horse when we went from full run to abrupt stop without warning.

I swallowed hard, unsure what to do as they stared at me, waiting.

We shouldn't split up, it could be another trick. The elves at Camber could handle the fey, would likely have it done before we arrived. But it wasn't right to leave them to it, either. I cursed myself for not having more animals at the castle. It would be all I needed to resolve the issue in a matter of minutes. Recruiting the cats had ended badly and I'd not wanted a repeat.

"Frey," Chevelle called and I grimaced, knowing I could wait no longer.

"Council trackers are stealing up the mountain. They are almost to the castle." I glanced at the others, who had backtracked when they'd heard the commotion of the sudden stop. "Anvil, Chevelle, with me. The rest of you go on. We will join you as soon as the castle is secure."

No one looked happy with the idea, but they nodded their assent.

"Rhys," I added, surprised at the intensity of my own voice, "save one for me."

They turned back to the path, resuming the run with a new drive. I dropped from my horse and ran, knowing Chevelle and Anvil would follow. They were faster, but I knew the secret paths and tunnels. We hadn't ridden far before I'd found the intruders, but hopefully any spotters thought we were well gone.

I cut from the path and through a narrow pass between boulders, climbed a rock wall, and slid behind a tattered group of thorn bushes before stopping to check the trackers' progress.

"There are four," I whispered. "One is scaling the north wall. Two outside the east wing… they appear to be waiting for a signal. The fourth is farther down, hiding among the rocks."

The instant my eyes opened, I was running again, darting through crevices and climbing over stone. I would lose the tracker once he was inside the castle walls, but I couldn't stay with him and keep moving. I had to figure out where he was going, what he wanted within. They knew we were gone, surely. They had waited for this opportunity. But why?

I slipped on a loose rock and narrowly caught myself in time. Cool moss beneath my palm signaled we were nearly there, and I glanced up, searching the wall for the entrance. I nodded, confident now, and Chevelle pulled a dagger from his belt as we began again. We were through the entry and sprinting down the dark corridor when I realized where the tracker was headed.

"The vault," I said, breathless from running.

Anvil cursed. "I'll take the two on the east wing. We'll catch the fourth before he swings back around. There's nowhere for him to go."

I nodded. "Here." It was the only warning I gave before throwing myself through the end wall where the corridor turned. I felt

Chevelle and Anvil falter at my use of magic, but they recovered quickly, Anvil splitting from us toward the east wing as we kept on for Asher's vault.

The hallway was too quiet. The pad of our boots seemed to thunder in the silence. But that didn't matter as soon as Chevelle busted the door to the vault. The seal had been broken, so he must have expected the tracker to replace it with a new one.

I couldn't worry about who the tracker had killed to get here, where the fallen might be, because once the door was open, flames burst into the hallway. They died down after a moment, and I could see Chevelle again, forced to the opposite side of the opening.

He gave me a look. *I thought you said they were trackers.* I turned my palms up. They had been dressed like trackers, they had moved like trackers. Someone with this kind of power shouldn't have bothered learning stealth.

The wall beside Chevelle blew out, large chunks of stone flying into the corridor, and he jumped back, pressed farther from me. Had Council been cross-training their strongest fighters all along, or had we given them too much time to regroup? The next blast opened the wall beside me and I leapt out of the way, flinching as pieces of rock pelted my side.

I glanced back at Chevelle, whose expression left no doubt he was about to pummel this nasty interloper. But just as he shifted to move on the entrance, a cyclone of paper, Asher's precious documents, swirled into the corridor. I bit down hard. This was one man. And we were wasting time.

I stepped in front of the opening in one swift move, just as Chevelle did the same. The documents parted—Chevelle's magic—and the tracker's arms and legs broke at the bicep and thigh—mine. He fell back against a shelf, gritted his teeth, and threw a vicious strike toward me, which met my power and dissolved to nothing. He threw another, and then another, to no avail. I stepped forward, ready to question him, and recognized his face. Archer Lake.

He smiled at my recognition. It was an ugly, hate-filled flash of teeth and I wanted to destroy it.

Flames returned with the memory. I felt the heat surround us as I watched her burn. He had been the one who'd finally overtaken her. They had all killed my mother, but this man had possessed the strength to overwhelm her, an energy of legend. He had burned her.

And he had taken pleasure in it.

I would make him suffer. He would blister and burn in agony. Dark hair whipped my face as I drew air into the room to feed the flame. He would boil. He would suffer. He threw another blast of power toward me, but I couldn't even feel it now, the collision was nothing. *He* was nothing.

"Frey!" Chevelle's voice cut through the anger, and I was startled by the inferno. We were surrounded by flame. Had he been yelling?

I glanced at him, beside me, unburned but clearly in pain, and shook myself. The fire extinguished while I let out a long breath, as if blowing out a flickering candle, as I released the magic. My eyes connected with Chevelle's and we stood for a moment, understanding passing between us. He was right. We had to get to Anvil.

I looked one last time at the man who had killed my mother. He was badly burned, but seemed relieved. As if he were saved now. I shook my head in disbelief and then severed the large vessels of his heart. He wouldn't die slow enough, but he would die.

19

MYST

We found Anvil among a pile of rubble that used to be the east wall. He was winded and between that and the chaos of stone, I knew the two here had been no mere trackers either.

"What happened?" I asked, glancing at the destruction surrounding us.

He shook his head. "Not trackers. They were waiting for whoever was inside to return." He took a deep breath. "They were going to ruin what they could of the castle and grounds."

I eyed the remaining section of wall. They hadn't done a bad job of it, even now.

A few sentries were running toward us, finally aware of the attack. I couldn't fault them, it had all happened rather quickly. Chevelle gave them a brief explanation and instructed them where to search for the fallen and what to repair first. I took the opportunity to find my hawk.

When I opened my eyes again, Anvil was recovered. "Where is the other one?"

"Hunkered down on the northeast crag. No doubt he heard

this"—I gestured toward the wall—"so he must have known better than to run."

"Or he has some agenda," Chevelle said.

I shrugged. "We can find them here or at the temple. It will end the same."

From the east tower, a sentry called out that he'd found a fallen comrade. The three of us looked toward the sound.

Chevelle's voice cut through the silence that followed. "Then let us end it."

We moved swiftly across the yard and down the jagged black rock to where I'd seen the Council member.

As we neared the target, Anvil shouted, "Show yourself."

There was no response, so we stepped carefully closer, the three of us spread out along the mountainside. I could barely see the colors of his robe where he'd concealed himself, and a surge of apprehension prickled my skin. This felt like a trap.

"Hold," Chevelle said from across the rock.

I glanced at him, and then heard the chanting. That wasn't fear prickling my skin, it was the edge of a spell. I stepped back involuntarily.

"You cannot protect yourself," Anvil called to the mass of rock. "Will you go out like a coward?"

The chanting grew louder and I had to fight not to move back again.

Anvil's gaze fell on Chevelle, silently questioning whether he recognized the words. Chevelle grimaced, the gesture conveying we'd not be able to cross the bounds of the protection spell. He glanced at me, and I immediately shook my head. There was no way I was going to let him battle a Council member with spellcasting.

I sat on the rock behind me, careful to secure my foothold among the looser pieces below my feet, and closed my eyes. It took longer than I would have liked, but I tried to focus solely on bringing the animal in with as much speed as possible instead of thinking about the attack on Camber, or that I should be with my guard, not here in the broken shards of the crag with a single Council member.

The cat had been hunting at the base of the cliffs, so it came from below us, agile form moving swiftly up the treacherous granite to the saw-toothed rock where we waited.

From that vantage point, I could see the man; it was Clay of Rothegarr. He had not bothered protecting the back side of his enclosure.

His face changed when he saw the golden fur of the mountain lion rushing toward him. It was some mixture of wonder and dread. He hurried to defend himself, drawing a thorn bush toward him and heaving as much energy as he could into expanding its size. The cat struck, clamping its strong jaw around the Council member's leg, and I could feel the muscles of his thigh tearing under the biting grip as he struggled against it. The cat hadn't been able to reach his neck in time, but this was instinct. It would wait for him to die, never easing its grip until it was over.

I felt my own body jerk as the thorns pierced the cat's hide. Through its eyes, I hadn't seen the vines growing, only the blood as it poured from the Councilman's wound and bubbled up beneath our muzzle. We bit harder, twisting, tearing, and lost our footing as the vines pushed us from the ground. A thorn ran through the pad of our paw, breaking through the top, and we yowled before striking again, but we missed, our jaw snapping shut against air as the vines caught our neck and held us in place. We struggled, furious and desperate, but the tree only tightened around us.

A hand on my shoulder, a word in my ear brought me back to my own body, gasping for air. *Right.* It was the cat. Not me.

"Can you get my lion out?" I whispered to Chevelle.

He knelt beside me. "Not without casting."

I swallowed hard, my throat dry, and then shook my head. It was too risky.

A high-pitched cry escaped the cat, now wounded and trapped within the thorn tree, and I acted without thought, placing my hands to the ground in front of me, cursing the Council member to death.

"Frey," Chevelle warned from beside me, moving to stand as the ground shook beneath us.

Rock crashed into rock as it tumbled down the steep mountainside and I could hear Anvil swear as he and Chevelle worked to protect us from the avalanche. But I couldn't stop. This was wrong. We shouldn't be here, trying to drive out this one remaining nuisance instead of fighting against Council in a proper clash. We had given them time to regroup and they were fighting dirty. Like the fey. The fey, who were, as we sat here, attacking Camber. We were being assailed from all sides when we should have been avenging the massacre, setting the wrong to right.

"Frey!" Chevelle's voice was a command this time as he grabbed me by the shoulders and hoisted me to standing. But I didn't fight him. I was done.

The mountain fell quiet as the final rock settled, and Chevelle spun me around to face him. He was angry, and I knew he'd intended to ask me what I thought I was doing, but whatever he saw in my expression stopped him.

"Is the casting broken?" I asked in a lifeless voice.

He nodded. We'd not been able to use magic within the boundaries of the spell, but the rock had made it through. Clay of Rothegarr was dead.

"Will you get my cat? We need to go."

He released my arms and I closed my eyes to call our horses to the castle. Rock clattered as Chevelle cleared the debris surrounding the thorn tree. I dropped quickly to the mind of the cat, willing it not to hurt Chevelle as he freed it.

We needed to get to Camber. We needed to end this. All of it.

I glanced at the sky as we rode for Camber. The sun was too low on the horizon, though we'd been running since we'd left the castle. Chevelle had carried the mountain lion to the yard, where he'd left instructions to build an enclosure for the animal and tend it as best as possible until Ruby had returned. We'd barely spoken since, nothing but the rhythmic thump of horse hooves on the path, until we neared the bounds of Camber.

"Is it safe?" Chevelle asked from his place behind me.

The heavens were empty, likely due to the fighting, so I drew a red-tail from its perch in the safety of a black spruce. There was nothing in the outlying crevices and copses. Nothing on the paths into town. Nothing, until my circles brought me closer to the epicenter, where smoke and dust rose in caustic clouds above Camber.

"It's over," I said, opening my eyes again to clear skies and order. "And I don't see anything lying in wait for us."

When we finally reached town, most of the major damage was restored. The ground was littered with fairy dust and bits of wing, pebbles and ash. A dozen busted wine casks were scattered in front of the Kraig residence, and the deep purple fluid splashed beneath our horses' hooves where it ran in rivulets over the dark stone path, trickling halfway through town before waning to nothing. Troughs were overturned, crowns of houses were lying in rubble on front porches, and horses were painted with berry juice and shimmer. But the fires were no longer burning, the floods had been diverted. No bodies lay in the street.

Rider met us near the center of town. I could tell by his appearance such had not been the case when they'd arrived.

"I suggest making your way to Ruby's house," he said. "It appears her protections worked quite nicely to deter the fey." He glanced around, clearly not wanting to voice the real reason in front of a crowd. "Rhys waits for you there."

I nodded, understanding his hesitation. They'd saved one, and by the looks of the elves here, they wanted no part of it.

"Is anyone hurt?" I asked.

"Ruby is tending them," he said. "Seems they've taken to her, here at least." He saw my uncertainty. "We have everything else under control." He was right, but it wasn't easy to walk away.

Rider glanced past me to Anvil. "What did you get into?"

I followed his gaze to find Anvil's forearm caked with blood. I'd not even noticed.

Anvil waved it off. "They weren't trackers. Sent some muscle to tear up things while we were down there looking for them."

I wondered briefly if there was more truth to his words than he realized. Council might not be at the temple at all. But I didn't mention it. This was no time for supposition. Chevelle and I left Anvil and Rider to exchange stories and assist the others. As we rode through Camber, the passing elves stopped to watch, a mixture of emotion meeting our presence.

Ruby's home stood out among the rest, clean of assault, and I had to wonder if it had been her protections as Rider had suggested, or if the fey had done this intentionally.

We stopped in front of the house where another horse stood, drinking from the only unmolested water trough in town. I stepped down, staring at the poor beast as it puffed into the water. A smattering of small handprints painted its ribcage while its mane stood in thick, gooey spikes. I shook my head; I would never understand their fixation with horses.

Chevelle waited for me at the door, where I took one deep breath before nodding for him to go on. We slipped in quickly, dreading what we'd find on the other side.

Ruby's living area seemed smaller, though I couldn't say whether it was owing to my memory or the pale blue fairy that hovered above the couch, flittering nervously from side to side.

"Myst," I sighed, undecided if I was relieved.

"Lord Freya," she crooned, "so good to have a friend here." Her expression was hopeful until she saw mine did not change, and then her shoulders fell.

I moved forward, taking a seat across from her as she dropped gracefully onto the couch. Her feet never touched the floor as her slender legs curled up beneath the wispy fabric of her skirts. The material would have been too fragile for most fey, but Myst was more than a few decades old. Not that anyone could tell by looking. The fey were ageless, growing to full maturity within a couple of years and remaining as such until death, which came by some means other than old age, more often than not.

I glanced briefly at Rhys, who appeared in fair condition. Myst would have been exceedingly well behaved in her current predicament. Given what she'd find outside, escape would be far worse than anything we could do to her.

She waited for me to speak, though anyone could see it pained her to stay still. One corner of her pale bottom lip was tucked under her teeth and she picked at the poppy seeds detailing her skirt. But her colorless eyes remained on me.

"Tell me you're not in league with Grand Council," I said.

She laughed, but it took on an uneasy stutter when she realized I was serious.

I leaned forward. "Why are you here? All of you?"

"We were supposed to have free rein once Council was removed." Her gaze flicked to Chevelle and then back to me. "You know, before someone called war."

I glared at her. We'd not even left the castle before they'd attacked, let alone given them reason to declare war.

She shrugged. "We got a little excited."

I stood, suddenly no longer able to bear being in the room, this situation.

She stood as well, slender, silk-covered feet landing noiselessly on stone. "What about me?"

I smiled. "You are free to go."

20

MESSENGERS

She wouldn't leave, I knew that, but I had to get away from her. So I was standing in Ruby's tiny guest room, staring blankly at my reflection in the large ornate mirror when Chevelle came in.

"You were right," I said numbly, unable to look at him as he approached to stand behind me.

He didn't speak.

"I was about to cause a war. A war we couldn't win." I looked down at my hands, feeling helpless at my lack of control. "I nearly set into motion a conflict that would all but hand our world to the fey."

His fingers slipped against my waist and the simple touch brought, if not relief, then reassurance. I turned to him, sliding my own hand up his arm, but when I finally looked into the deep sapphire of his eyes, all I could think was, *What now?*

"Freya," he started, but I cut him off.

"What is it?"

He held up a scroll with his other hand. "A messenger was here."

I took two sideways steps to sit on the bed, not positive I could remain standing when he told me who'd been lost. "Who?"

"Two watchmen, a sentry, and a keep. The sentry was of Camber, the second messenger is with his family now."

They had killed four. Masquerading as trackers, they had snuck onto the grounds, taking down anyone who'd seen them. Archer had attempted to steal the casting ledgers from the vault while the rest lay in wait. To burn and raze the castle.

I was abruptly standing again. Chevelle saw my fury, but he didn't attempt to calm it. This would have to be answered for, if not now, then soon. The realization eased my temper enough that I could at least consider our options.

I began pacing. Asher had never allowed me to pace. It was a weakness, he'd said. But he was dead.

"I should see the family," I said, a plan forming. It wasn't a solid plan. It was based purely on faith, but it was a plan. And it was the only one I had.

Chevelle nodded. "As will I. Burne has a grown son. His wife is Camren. She's known for her talent with wind."

I came to a standstill, straightening my scabbard before gripping the hilt of my sword. "Yes, we will see her first." My eyes met Chevelle's but before I could decide whether to tell him, there was a crash from the front room.

I bit down a growl, muttering, "I hate fairies," for what was almost certainly not the last time as I opened the door to the living area.

The pale blue fairy was perched on the arm of the sofa by the tips of her toes. Her hands were behind her back and she wore an all-too-innocent smile as she greeted me in singsong. "Frey-a."

I grimaced at her as I asked Rider, "What did she break?"

He nodded toward the corner, where a gooey mess oozed from broken chunks of what I assumed was once a clay pot. "Not sure exactly, but it smells like the back end of a goat."

Myst grinned wider, as if her perfect teeth could charm me into friendship.

"Clean it up and I will let you live."

She started to laugh but caught herself, unsure if I'd been joking. Her wings flicked, shaking silvery dust onto the couch, and then she moved to pick up the mess.

I headed to Ruby's room to locate a scroll and then stood frozen in the doorway. The entire room was covered in a thick white powder. "What happened?" I managed, choking on fumes even though the dust had long since settled.

"Oh," Rider said, "that was Ruby."

I turned to stare at him.

"One of the traps she'd laid before leaving."

I pointed a thumb over my shoulder, face blank as his words sunk in.

"Yep, that's the one that got Steed."

The laugh that escaped morphed into a cough from the vapor and I closed the door without having stepped a foot inside. My eyes were tearing up. No wonder he'd been so angry. "Any chance either of you have a scroll and a quill?"

"Here," Myst called from the corner, "there are some in this side table."

I glanced at Chevelle, who had the same irritated expression I imagined I was wearing, and headed toward the table.

Myst stood. "And a jar of ink there." She pointed toward a row of shelves built into the south wall, where it appeared she had been meddling when she'd knocked down the clay pot. "It's the blue one." Nose scrunched, she bent back to her task.

When I pulled a scroll from the drawer, she glanced up at me, eyebrows dancing up and down. "Writing a missive?"

I narrowed my eyes on her and she smiled sweetly before wiping the remaining goo from the floor.

Sitting in the chair opposite the couch, I slid a small table to me and laid out the scroll. Myst sat the jar of ink beside it without a word and moved across from me, curling her feet under and resting her elbows on a couch pillow in her lap while she watched. It wouldn't matter, she'd read it as soon as she was out of my sight, but I took the time to glare at her anyway, blowing the bangs out of my eyes as I looked up from the table at her. She didn't seem to mind, bringing her tiny fists up to rest under her chin as she waited. Her soft blue-gray locks fell forward in loose waves and the color reminded me of the sky just before rain. It seemed apt, considering the storm I was about to unleash.

I had the first line down when Ruby came in. Her face was smudged with dust and blood, and fuzzy tendrils of red curled around it where they'd escaped her braid. She stared blankly at the blue fairy roosting on her couch, and then at me.

"Is everything well, Ruby?" I asked.

"I've done all I can." She sighed. "I'm going to clean up."

I nodded, hoping she remembered the explosion of powder waiting in her room.

I was on the last line when Grey came in. I glanced up just in time to see his eyes meet Myst's. She let out a cat-like "reouw" sound and sat straight up to get a better look at him. Grey, along with the rest of us, simply stared in open shock at her display.

When Ruby appeared from nowhere and leapt at her, Myst only had time to half turn toward her as she collided into the fairy and both rolled across the floor beside me. I heard an oath, recognized it as Grey, and realized he'd joined the fracas, struggling unsuccessfully to pull Ruby from her victim. Another curse flew out as Myst scratched his cheek in an attempt to gouge his eye, and I slowly became aware that I and the remaining members of the guard were simply watching as this bizarre scuffle ensued. Before I was able to react though, Ruby drove her forehead into Myst's petite nose and flipped her face-first onto the ground. My mouth popped open as Ruby pinned her, pulled Myst's wrists together behind her back, and leaned forward to whisper into a long, pointed ear.

Whatever she said made Grey flush as red as one of Ruby's silk scarves and I flashed a look to Chevelle to see if he'd heard. His eyes were on Grey, jaw tight with restraint as he held back laughter.

"Ruby," I said, staring down at her, "I need this one."

She nodded, pushing roughly off Myst's back to stand.

I leaned over the scroll to sign my name, not as Veil and the fey called me, but as Elfreda, Lord of the North. Myst sat up, wiping the blood that ran from her busted nose, and handed me a ribbon and seal as if nothing was out of the ordinary.

I rolled the parchment slowly, considering my words. Part bluff, part bravado, part outright deceit. I could only hope it worked. Veil was no fool, but I had to believe he didn't want war. There was no other reason to warn me. Well, there was one other reason, but I refused to think of that now that I knew I was tied to Chevelle. It would have to work. I wrapped the ribbon once around the document, attached the seal, and pressed the clasp of my cloak into the clay putty, the molded form of a hawk imprinted as my seal.

Myst leaned forward, blew gently onto the putty, and smiled as it hardened to ceramic. She rolled to her knees, eagerly awaiting her instructions.

"Deliver this to Veil."

She nodded. "And you'll get me out of here alive?"

I knew what she meant. Could I get her safely out of Camber? Would these men heed my orders? I didn't have the slightest idea, but at least she had enough respect not to say it.

I rubbed my face. "You'll leave with us. It's the best I can do."

She pursed her lips, another unspoken question. Where were we going?

"We will keep the balance, that is all that matters. Tell him we planned to return to the castle."

For the first time, a truly sincere smile crossed her lips. That was when I knew we were in more trouble than we could handle.

I stood to address the guard. "We leave at daybreak. Please let Steed and Anvil know. We won't have much time to wrap things up." I indicated Chevelle. "We are going to pay our respects to Camren. When we return"—I glanced at Myst—"we will discuss strategy."

As we made our way to the door, I realized I hadn't known Burne. I wondered briefly where we'd find his wife, what condition she'd be in. But as soon as Chevelle drew the door open, it became quite apparent where she was, if not her condition.

Marching toward Ruby's small home was a band of angry townspeople. They were dressed in battle gear, armor and swords, knives and shields. Their faces were smeared with the blood of the fey, their hands clenched upon hammers and axes.

And leading the pack was a stout woman in her fourth century, dark eyes rimmed in red, mouth taut with determination and pain.

"Camren?" I whispered.

"Yes," Chevelle answered behind me.

I took a deep breath, watching as the woman's raven hair whipped in a around her.

The group came to a staggered stop as they reached the street in front of the house. There were about thirty, a few kneeling to show respect, a few rocking impatiently from foot to foot, but most standing in wait as Camren approached further. I stepped onto the porch and Chevelle followed, coming to stand beside me. Rhys and Grey came to my right, and I heard the door shut behind them, locking the fairy away from view.

"You go to take your vengeance?" Camren asked in a raw voice.

Her question left no room for the indecision I was feeling. "The fey attacked this town because of our plan to confront Council."

Camren's jaw went tight. "Do you go to take your vengeance?"

"Retaliation could mean war," I said.

Three of the large elves behind her spat at my answer, several others muttered. They had no fear of the fey, and Council had taken one more of their own today. One too many, it appeared.

I sighed. "Many of you will die."

No one in the line so much as flinched at my words. From the corner of my eye, I saw Steed and Anvil approaching to join us. Not an hour ago, I'd been questioning my actions, convinced I'd made a poor choice, that I would have started a war not only the north, but the whole of elvinkind would lose. Now, I could see no other way.

I glanced at Chevelle, and knew he felt the same. It was right. We would have to do it, regardless of the cost.

When I gave the order, I stared solely into Camren's eyes. A promise. "Then we go. Recompense for the fallen." I looked past her then, into the eyes of the men and women behind her. "Not just for today, but for all days. These men will answer for their actions."

A clatter of sword against shield met my words, the applause of battle, and I looked to my guard. We were ready.

21

RECKONING

The fey attack and the trackers had thrown our plans into chaos. But the gathering outside Ruby's door added urgency. We would have no time to revise our strategy or we would risk giving Council notice, not to mention a return of the fey. So I had decided to tell the mob of townspeople of my messenger, and trust them to allow her departure.

But when I opened the door to the living area and her gaze skipped over the crowd to land directly on the horses with a giddy, "Oooh, do I get one?" I considered letting them rip her apart. Unfortunately, I couldn't chance sending anyone else into fey territory under the current conditions.

"Go now or not at all, fairy," I hissed below earshot, and then bit my cheek as she curtseyed for the spectators.

Myst beamed at me before dipping and shoving off the porch to disappear about as quickly as I'd ever seen a fey disappear, excepting Veil, of course.

Straightening my shoulders, I took one more look around before calling the order to mount up. We had split the group into five. I would ride with the guard as we had intended, as if we were alone. Two sets of Camber's best horsemen would ride slightly eastern and western routes, and the last two, the strongest and fastest, would come in on foot. It wasn't the most honest formation, but they'd played dirty first, and I didn't aim to lose any more men than necessary.

We rode swiftly and silently. I spent most of the ride falling into the minds of various birds in an effort to keep us safe. There had been a fair share of attempts on me, the guard, and the north of late so I couldn't be sure of what exactly I was looking for, but nothing seemed amiss. It was maybe too calm. It reminded me of the ice attack. Nothing to be seen, nothing out of place.

The train of thought distracted me as I scanned the grounds below. I didn't need to be distracted, so I forced myself to stop worrying about Veil. Stop worrying about how I could control these powers. I needed to focus on our current task. To overcome this one obstacle first.

Back to myself, I glanced left and right to find Steed and Chevelle. Chevelle's eyes were scanning the trees, Steed's moving from the landscape, over the horses, and back again. Rhys and Rider rode ahead, Ruby, Grey, and Anvil behind. I checked on the horses, wondering how much farther they could run, but it seemed we might not have to continue on foot. Chevelle had been right, they were fine stock.

We didn't slow through the darkness of night. The cool air seemed to recharge the horses, and their excitement recalled old memories to me.

I could hear the purr of breath, see the black coat glisten over straining muscle through the blur of ash and tears. The stench of burning flesh still remained in my nose and throat, the screams of so many still echoed through my mind. My ears roared with some unknown resonance. All I could do was hold on to Chevelle's back, though I wanted nothing more than to tear everything apart.

My mother's words sang softly to me, a warning, just before I was attacked. A deep green vine rose to strike, curling like a viper, and shot out, thorns piercing my arms like fangs as its rapidly growing body wrapped around my wrist in a choking hold.

"Frey."

I jerked awake, so suddenly pulled from the dream that I struggled against Chevelle's grip on my arm.

"Freya," he repeated.

I sputtered, yanked my arm once more, and then finally breathed. He watched me, only releasing his hold when it was clear I had my bearings.

"Thank you," I whispered in a hoarse voice, at last realizing I'd fallen asleep as we rode.

His head tilted forward, and I followed it to find the familiar rocks marking the way to the temple. It was time.

We dismounted and as Steed turned the horses to graze, I took one last trip to the sky to be certain everyone was in place.

I opened my eyes to find seven soldiers watching me. I gave them one nod that I hoped conveyed everything and took my first step toward River Temple.

Two hundred steps later, the trees took on a new appearance. Great oaks and maples grew vigorously, limbs overlapping as their massive trunks stood too close together. The excess of leaves created a low canopy of dappled green, out of season with the cool air. We continued through the maze wordlessly, treading lightly and on watch. We had no guarantee they weren't lying in wait.

When the forest border began to clear, my guard took up lines. Rhys and Rider led as Chevelle and Anvil flanked me. Ruby, Steed, and Grey walked behind, rotating to watch our backs and the sky. After their attack on the castle, we were sure they would try again. But they weren't waiting for us in the surrounding forest. They were waiting for us in the temple.

Seventy white robes lined the temple floor. Twenty more were staggered between the sandstone columns. Three and thirty stood along the balcony railing. Bright eyes and golden hair were all that set them apart at that instant. Gone was their jovial mood. No one smiled now.

My eyes scanned the room, searching. The floor was nothing but fodder. Single tassels adorned most robes; none there wore more than three. These were fresh recruits, brought in to wear us down. A few among the columns might be able to contest the townspeople, but held no threat to my guard.

The balcony. That was where our targets waited. They watched us, no hint of wariness, only pure hatred. They thought us evil. They thought to take our lands, destroy our people. They had bound me. They had burned my mother.

The ground shook. It was only when Chevelle's hand touched the small of my back that I realized the tremor came from me. I had to control Asher's magic. It was too much to release in overwhelming anger. It would consume us.

"Elfreda of Camber," the Council speaker called from the balcony.

I stopped him before he could finish his speech. "It is *Lord* Freya."

He set his jaw. "We of the Council of the Order of the Light Elves…"

I glanced at Chevelle. They would proclaim their innocence, their rightfulness, play out this display in front of the new members. In front of those who didn't know the truth.

They intended to win.

They didn't expect those on the floor to live, but they were covering their tracks in case a few survived before wearing us down. The seven of my guard. And me.

I stepped forward. "Your words waste your final breath. We come to avenge the lives of the lady Eliza"—I let my gaze trail the balcony—"of Rosalee of Camber"—Steed stiffened beside me at the mention of his mother, but I carried on—"of all the mothers of the North."

I lost their attention for a moment, and knew the warriors of Camber had arrived to our right. Camren would be among them. "We come to avenge the lives of Burne, and all the husbands of the North."

The thrum of beating hooves followed and all eyes fell to the approaching horses behind us. "We come to avenge the honor of our lands, of our people. We come to avenge our lives."

At this, three Council members on the upper level stepped back, but I only smiled. The fourth band of Camber warriors waited behind the temple.

"What say you, speaker?"

I had anticipated some hesitation at the sight of the additional fighters, but there was none. What was left of this Council had decided to end the North, and they apparently had no notion that they might lose.

Their first strike was swift and severe. Some unseen signal unleashed a hail of fire, exploding light, and countless bursts of energy. There would be no weapons here. The Council members on the floor would be instructed to kill or die. They would have no second chance.

There was a thundering response from our line and nearly a third of the seventy went down. In a matter of minutes, the few who remained pushed back behind the columns where the second line of attack waited. They worked together to bring the water. The resounding roar was accompanied by a vibration, which quickly grew to shake dust from the columns of the temple.

When the wave crashed onto the floor beneath the balcony, the Camber lines stepped back. They had called the river on us, and it was coming with no sign of restraint. A wall of water rolled toward us with the force of two dozen's magic. I raised my hands, wondering if I could release enough power to stop it without harm to myself or my guard.

Chevelle called out an order to the lines beside me, but the sound was lost as a violent wind struck the wave with a boom that reverberated through the room. The water fought against the barrier, stopped in its advance mid-crash as it hung before us. It had happened so fast, it took my mind a moment to catch up.

"Push back," I yelled, releasing only a portion of the strike I had planned to unleash. As soon as the wave fell back into a flood, I searched the line for Camren, but it was too late. Her body lay motionless on the ground. She'd given her last breath for this retaliation. Two villagers moved to kneel beside her and I looked back just in time to see the water wash over the temple floor, flushing at least a handful of Council members with it as it crossed between the columns and out of the structure.

We surged forward then, taking the last of those Council members to leave only thirty remaining above. The leaders of Grand Council.

"*Dratva Sprego Drangia Rema.*"

The words fell from the balcony, heavy with a vow of devastation, and I looked up to find their source. It was Elden of Longarten, the man who'd set fire to the gates of the castle during the massacre. They'd not wanted anyone to escape. They'd wanted all of us to burn.

Like my mother.

As the spell took hold of the others, fury spread through my veins like that fire so long ago. Hot, burning anger devoured every part of me until it seemed to burst, snapping any connection I had to calm, rational thought. If the ground shook again, I did not feel it. If the spell attempted to harm me, I did not know. The only thing there was was rage.

I stared into the eyes of my mother's killers as the stone cracked and split.

I saw Nyle, who had drowned the young sentry in his own blood.

I saw Sandon, who had slowly choked the serving girls with bay vine while chaos reigned around them.

I saw Fawn, who had opened the chests of the watchmen, a smile playing at the corner of her honey-rose lips as their insides spilled onto the castle floor.

I watched as the balcony gave way.

I watched as they fell with the floor beneath them.

A cloud of dust rose as the heart of the temple crumbled onto the ground in front of us. Lightning flashed and thunder boomed. The wind whipped as though a hurricane centered among the columns. Fire and screams tore through the air in a battle so reminiscent of the massacre, it made my chest hurt. But the knowledge of this final revenge didn't ease the pain. Even as those who were guilty took their dying breaths, the ache only grew.

Body after body fell. What remained of the fourth line advanced, and we surrounded the last of the Council leaders. A flash of light shot out, intense enough to bring me from the trance of anger that had destroyed the temple. I was moving but Rider was faster. He threw himself forward to let loose an explosion of power so violent it seemed to burn my skin.

Wincing against the flare, I turned back to see it strike its target and issued an attack of my own. They were few now, but they were strong. Twin blows punched my chest but I pushed them back before they could tear me apart. Anvil stepped in front of me just in time to catch a third, and I felt a jolt as it collided with his shoulder.

Chevelle moved forward then, as we all advanced on them, and deflected two more before Rhys and Rider moved to the front. Their skill was incredible as they pooled their energy to defend and attack. I shifted to throw another strike, but faltered when Ruby fell beside me.

I had to force myself not to reach for her. Her red curls had slipped loose of their binding and dropped onto the temple floor, now muddy with dust and blood, as she'd collapsed. I could not reach for her. I had to keep fighting.

My feet were frozen, afraid to disturb what lay beneath me as my eyes fell again on the enemy. The ache in my chest had intensified, risen to choke me. I could not bear to think of the possibilities, could only attempt to channel the hurt and anger.

I swayed, the power roiling through me, searching for escape, and the others turned, as if sensing the change.

Energy cracked through me and I nearly lost the capacity for control. I felt myself begin to lurch forward, but somehow held fast, just long enough to discharge the shattering force. Eyes narrowed, willing myself to focus, I watched as something inside them seemed to burst.

There were no more. They had all fallen.

The realization found me keeled over, braced against my wavering knees. For one long moment, my eyes were closed. For that moment, I felt as if my world might fragment, as if my being might dissolve. As if my insides might find their way out.

I managed a shallow breath against my tight chest and let it out without gagging. I opened my eyes to find Ruby staring up at me from the ground at my feet.

"Huh," she coughed.

I didn't know if the sound was impressed or stunned, but I choked out something like a laugh as I fell to my knees with relief.

22

SUMMONING

I watched numbly as Grey carried Ruby away. They'd assured me she wasn't terribly hurt, but it was obvious she wasn't terribly all right either. Blood had smeared her face and shallow breaths had wheezed out of her.

My hands were still wet from lifting her matted curls from the muddy floor. There would be blood on them. Not hers. The lifeblood of the men and women of Camber.

I started when something brushed my arm, but quickly relaxed when the warmth of a familiar hand settled onto the small of my back. I gave Ruby one more moment before turning my gaze to Chevelle beside me.

His deep blue eyes were intense, questioning and comforting at the same time. We had done it, we had crushed this one obstacle. We had avenged my mother, the north. But it had cost us. I stared back at him, hoping to convey my answers, to offer him some comfort in return, and he reached up to place his palm against my cheek. I closed my eyes, breathed deep for the first time since the battle, and felt the last of the trembling in my limbs subside.

When I opened my eyes again, Chevelle slid his hand free, brushing the damp from my cheek, and we turned to survey the damage.

River Temple lay in ruin. Half of the columns were rubble. The rest were covered in ivies as the Council members had tried to elevate themselves above the flood waters. Patches of floor had dried from the winds, dust and blood, leaving rust-colored stains. In a matter of weeks, the damage would look centuries old.

Several men were climbing over the remains of the balcony where it lay on the ground, searching the dead. I didn't need to check, their faces were seared into my memory. What I was concerned about, however, was our men. From our position at the front of the line, we hadn't been able to see who'd been injured.

I scanned the area, surprised to find that most of the wounded were already being tended. A few of the Camber warriors were limping or bloodied, but the majority of them appeared well. They had taken their place among the front, but Council had targeted the townspeople anyway. I tried not to count as I watched them being carried away, but I couldn't help it. Fourteen dead.

And Camren among them.

We approached the marble tablet where Bayrd and Emeline were cleaning up the injured.

Bayrd looked up from his work. "Lord Freya." He dipped his head respectfully, causing his patient to flinch as he pulled against the stitches. He smirked before deference fell back in place to address Chevelle. "Excellent battle."

I glanced at Chevelle, but he didn't seem as surprised as I was to find them in such good spirits.

The large, leather-clad elf beside him called out as Emeline set his shoulder back in place. "There you are, good as new," she promised. He didn't appear to believe her, but he stood, shrugged his shoulders twice, and dipped his head toward Chevelle and me before leaving.

Emeline turned to us. "That about finishes things up here." She glanced toward the clearing the warriors had made. "Except for the ceremony."

Bayrd tightened his last stitch.

"I'd like a messenger to notify the villagers. Some of them will have family here," I said.

Emeline nodded. "Merek will go. He's a fast rider." She eyed the afternoon sky. "Likely he could make the rounds before dawn."

"Thank you," I said.

She smiled. "Lord Freya."

Emeline brushed past me, and by the time I'd turned around, Merek was mounted and kicking a slender black stallion up to running.

All evidently taken care of, we went to find Ruby.

The task was easier than expected, because we could hear her fighting with Grey before we took the first step into the forest.

"I *said* I was fine," she argued in a raspy voice. The declaration was punctuated by the sound of her slapping his ministrations away.

There was a sharp gasp as he ignored her assertions and pressed against a wound. And then a low curse from Grey as she retaliated.

We came through the trees to find Anvil sitting on a stump laughing while a grim-faced Steed attempted to hold her still.

"Touch me one more time," she warned the both of them, "and you will pay."

Grey held out a finger, considering, and she narrowed her gaze on him. Steed's mouth screwed up as he waited, clearly reassessing his position.

"Ruby," I cut in, "are you well?"

She shrugged Steed's hands free. "Yes. Quite."

I felt my chest ease a bit, though she still looked a little pale. I glanced at Grey who, while annoyed, no longer seemed fearful.

"Great," I said. "Clean yourself up. We've got a ceremony to attend."

She smirked at Steed before turning an eyebrow up at Grey, daring him to challenge her.

Anvil laughed again.

The ceremony was completed as the sun fell beneath the horizon. We stood in full dress as the flames licked the air and trailed smoke into the twilight sky. The others would see it. The families of the Council members would know we had lost people as well. But there would be nothing left but ash.

As I watched the fire dance, I could not help but think of my mother. She had burned with no honor. But I could lay her to rest now. When the blaze subsided, I could let this go. This battle was over. The fire that had haunted me for so long would be gone.

I closed my eyes and breathed deep, letting the sharp scent of night flowers on the wind cut through the last of the acrid smoke. But it was only the briefest reprieve, because when I opened them again, I saw a warning flicker among the trees.

I felt my jaw tighten, but held fast. It would wait. We would see the ceremony through.

As the final ember darkened, I looked to my guard. They were still, somber, and had apparently not noticed our audience.

I waited until the first shifting boot sounded before directing Steed to ready the horses. He moved to do so without reservation, but I saw the question on the others' faces.

"We will not ride back to Camber," I answered. I glanced to the trees, searching for sign of any remaining fey. "There isn't time."

The townspeople were preparing for their own return, but I was certain they would make it to Camber safely. It had only been a scout. A warning.

"Are you sure?" Ruby asked, inspecting them skeptically as they packed their weapons and armor.

I wasn't sure.

"They are loyal," Rhys said. "With this, you have won their trust."

Anvil shifted, still favoring his injured shoulder. "Aye. You have them."

I nodded, watching a limping Bayrd climb onto his horse. I could only hope they were right. But it didn't matter. "We have no other choice."

"Where do we ride, then?" Anvil asked.

I sighed heavily before answering. "Junnie."

There was no doubt they were concerned by my words, but the set of my shoulders, the way my eyes scanned the trees, made it clear now was not the time to discuss it.

"I will inform the others," Chevelle said, heading toward Emeline and her husband.

"Shall we gather the scrolls?" Ruby asked.

"No, leave those for the villagers," I said. "They are of no use to anyone now." I forced a smile. "You fought well, Ruby."

She was caught off guard. Her expression fell blank. "Did I?"

I nodded, and then cuffed her on the back. "Next time try to take no more than your share."

From the corner of my eye, I saw Anvil's mouth tweak up in amusement.

Steed rode up then, mounted on a fine black stallion, and tilted his head toward the waiting group of horses. "They are fresh, ready for whatever you've got planned."

I resisted the urge to sigh again. "Thank you," I said, glancing over my shoulder for Chevelle.

"Here," he said from beside me, a large satchel over his shoulder. He saw me looking. "The townspeople wish you well and have sent provisions so that we may travel speedily."

My eyes narrowed on him. How would they know what we needed? But he only shrugged.

Steed called the horses to us, and as I swung onto my own, several of the townspeople bowed their respect. Among them, one form stood out.

Cold dark eyes met mine before a gloved hand raised in a gesture that vowed success. It was Camren's son.

I tried not to dwell on that gaze as we rode, but images of the battle were all I could seem to replace it with. The cool night turned to day, but even the sun didn't warm us. Camren had fallen. Avenging her husband, the boy's father. Wind had saved us from the wall of water, I reminded myself, saved the boy as well. And Camren's lifeless body had lain among the rest as the fires set them to rights.

Anvil's body took another hit as I relived the fight, and Steed's face twisted as pain cut through him. And then Ruby stared blankly up at me, the blood and mud surrounding her so dark against her pale skin. I shook myself, glancing again at her to confirm she was fine, her cheeks flushed, her emerald eyes clear and bright.

Looking ahead once more, I saw Rhys and Rider leading and remembered their fearless efforts. It was as if I could see the power move between them, seamlessly shifting where it was needed.

"Freya." Ruby's voice cut my reverie and I was startled to realize how deeply I'd fallen from the others.

I blinked, and she smiled. I was pretty sure she was laughing at me. The sky was overcast, hiding what I estimated to be a noon sun. "Yes, Ruby?"

"Are you going to tell us where we're going?" she whispered.

"We have to find Junnie."

She waited. She already knew that.

I couldn't stop myself from glancing around before answering. "We may have a slight problem," I said.

Ruby's brows shifted in a "what's new" motion.

I watched Chevelle as I continued, and it dawned on me that he didn't seem as anxious or surprised by my revelation. I guessed he'd seen the visitor as well. "There was a scout at the ceremony. A fire sprite, I think."

Ruby's nose crinkled. "Are you sure? Maybe it was just drawn to the action."

I shook my head. "No. It was a warning."

"But I thought you sent a message to Veil," she said.

"I did." I met her gaze evenly. "That's why we have to find Junnie."

Her brows drew together as she opened her mouth for another question, but a sudden call stopped her short.

It was the wolves.

23

UNEXPECTED

Suddenly, the rhythmic thump of our horses' hooves turned to the hammering of drums as they pounded the dirt in a full run. The wind caught my cloak to whip behind me and I held fast, closing my eyes to find the wolves. My mind brushed theirs before reaching a falcon tucked within the cover of a tall pine near them.

They were running.

I swung wide, searching for their prey, then behind, for an attacker. When I realized they weren't being pursued but coming for us, the falcon swooped down in front of them so they would know I'd found them. But instead of stopping to wait for us, they turned to run in the opposite direction. I opened my eyes.

I called out, "West," and the others adjusted their course without slowing. We ran through the forest, dodging brush and low limbs, and then into another clearing before we began to catch them.

"What is it?" Chevelle yelled.

I shook my head. "I don't know. They are alone."

And then we saw the smoke.

"There," Rider shouted as his horse narrowly avoided a thin oak.

We broke into a short clearing in time to see Finn and Keaton rushing through the trees ahead. At the next clearing, we saw why.

A large circle of ash covered the ground before us. Smoldering stumps and scattered embers were all that remained of a copse of what had been, from the smell, maple trees. It had burned fiercely, gone barely before we'd seen the smoke. The section of trees had been destroyed cleanly, nothing around it was disturbed, but another copse was already burning.

I scanned the scene as we ran, as we kicked up gray dust that still held heat, and saw two more patches of ash lay to the north. Understanding was slow to come. Someone was burning the forest in some systematic way. Just south of us, two more pillars of smoke rose, but Finn and Keaton took us north of the older fires.

The underbrush became dense, and the horses struggled through briars and thickets. They'd been fresh when we'd left the temple, but they were nearly finished now, drawing deep, purring breaths as sweat drenched their overworked bodies. Thunder rumbled in the distance and I glanced up at the darkening sky.

A break in the brush revealed an area of smooth rock where the wolves waited for us. They stood, chests heaving, tongues lolling to the side, and I was struck suddenly with the utter transformation—I'd never before seen them so wholly animal. How long had they been running?

The eight of us swung from our horses, landing on the flat stones of a now dry spring, and moved to stand before their silvery-gray forms. Finn nodded toward Rhys, and the two were off, running swift and silent through the trees beside us. They were headed for the fires. After some signal from Keaton, Steed sent the horses farther north, away from the blazes. The echo of cracking limbs and falling timbers muffled their escape, but the wind picked up and even the sounds of destruction were overcome by the rustling leaves surrounding us.

Chevelle moved beside me, as uneasy as the rest of us at the unknown, and we watched Keaton. He stood still now, eyes closed in some strange meditation, and I wondered if he was in the mind of his brother. I closed my own eyes, searching the forests, but the birds were gone, fled from the danger. A light brush of something else distracted me, but then my eyes shot open at the sound of a snapping branch nearby.

Finn burst back into the opening, Rhys steps behind.

"Rowan," Rhys said. "They've found Rowan and he's hunting Junnie, trying to burn her out."

"What? Why?" I stammered.

Rhys shook his head. "I don't know, but he's cursing her to the flames. He's vowed to kill her."

Chevelle stiffened. "Is he alone?"

"No," Rhys answered. "We couldn't get close enough to see without being spotted, but he's definitely got at least one ally with him. He was shouting orders."

Keaton growled.

I glanced briefly at the wolf as my next question came. "Why isn't she fighting? Or running?"

Anvil stepped forward. "If she were pinned down, that filthy son of an imp wouldn't be burning these groves."

"So he doesn't know where she is," Rider said. "But why is she hiding?"

Finn pawed the ground at my feet with an insistence that made me pause. I cursed.

The others focused on me, plainly unsure what to make of it. "The baby," I explained. "Junnie's protecting the human."

"Why would Rowan care about the baby?" Steed asked.

My brows pulled together, but before I could answer, an explosion of flame erupted less than a hundred yards south of us.

A furry shoulder nudged my leg and I glanced down at Finn. He was trying to tell me something, but the brush of something against my mind prickled my skin.

"We have to get Junnie," I said, ignoring the worry snaking its way through my gut. Before the others had a chance to respond, I was running toward the flames.

I could hear the others behind me, following as I bore down on that connection. It was different, less lucid and harder to grasp, but I could pin down its location. *Her* location.

Keaton bounced in front of me as we ran, but I didn't slow. There was an urgency now, a strong sense of pain and fear coming through the link. I had to get to them. Flames erupted beside us, and I heard the voice. Rowan called to Junnie, taunting her with death and suffering. He couldn't be more than a hundred yards from us, and Junnie was hiding in between.

It was surprising Rowan hadn't found her already, but from the sound of his tirade, he'd clearly been driven to madness. He must have been pushed; something must have caused him to break. I thought of the wolves and their recent absence just as they leapt to a stop in front of me, muzzles pulled back in a snarl.

I stopped, crouched down, and turned my face away as the blaze exploded before us.

"There," I whispered, staring back into the flames. "Junnie is in there."

Without a word, Ruby vaulted over the brush and into the mass of trees. Junnie had formed them perfectly, a natural barrier of oak and pine so solid they would have to be destroyed to reach her. And they were being destroyed now.

Heat burned my face as the smoke and flame rose. Rowan's voice echoed through what was left of the forest, promising Junnie's death to the inferno. I wanted to shut him up. Permanently.

Two more heartbeats and the flames began to waver. I took a breath, knowing Ruby had her. Had them. Chevelle's hand grasped my arm, but I couldn't look away. I had to be sure.

The instant Ruby pushed through the trees, the rest of us turned to run. The blaze had parted for her, obeying her talent as water on a current, and she broke through with Junnie in tow. The bundle in Junnie's arms was safe, though mildly singed , and the relief at knowing Junnie was alive was only surpassed by the relief of finally knowing she wasn't the one. Junnie had not been a part of the attacks on me; all doubt over the responsible party was gone. And my bargain with Veil would be a good one.

I wasn't certain where we were running to, where Rhys and Rider were leading us, but as we crossed a low ridge, two massive silver wolves crashed into me, knocking me solidly off my feet. We were not airborne for long, as my back slammed into a bank of dirt, eighty pounds of Keaton's furry body landing on top of me. He chuffed, I gasped, and we both rolled to the side to cough air back into our lungs.

A kind of roar escaped someone on the ridge, and I forced my head up to find Chevelle. He stood before a barrier of flame, which I assumed was more of Rowan's doing until I saw Ruby. Her body was rigid as she poured so much power into the wall, though I couldn't bring my mind to comprehend her motives. A soft whine came from the wolf beside me and I followed his gaze to find Finn lying still among the ground ivy.

I crawled to him, relieved to see his chest heave with breath, and ran my hand over his side, searching for broken bones. Finn's head raised, the silver-blue of his eyes meeting mine with more emotion than any ordinary beast could hold, and I understood. He'd taken a strike.

His nose twitched and pointed toward his shoulder. I brushed the fur aside, searching for the wound. There was a clean, small puncture directly beside the bone. I stared back into his eyes, knowing the pain I would cause when I turned him over, and lifted his legs to roll the other shoulder free. I glanced over my own shoulder, finding Keaton's back to me as he stood guard. Anvil and Grey remained on the ridge by Ruby, Rhys and Chevelle were running toward us.

As I looked down once more, my hand crossed the point of something sharp on Finn's side. I pulled my hand back, pressing the finger I'd pricked, and a drop of blood formed over the ash from Finn's coat. I looked up at Chevelle as his boots landed beside me and he bent down to slide a hand around the base of my arm. But he wasn't looking at the blood. He was looking at Rhys, who now held the weapon that had pierced Finn's shoulder. The bitter tang of poison reached me through the shock, and my stomach turned as I stared at the spear of steeled ice.

24

BLOOD AND BONE

The hand gripping my arm pulled me to standing and Chevelle pressed my finger to his mouth. He turned his head and spat, and then nodded once, apparently satisfied it had not tasted of poison.

He glanced over my shoulder at Rhys. "Move him to the pines. We will free Ruby."

My mind whirled, attempting to catch up, and I realized why Ruby had created a wall of fire. My feet were moving without thought. Finn would need her. We would face the ice.

"Ruby," I shouted over the noise. Wind whipped the top of the ridge, and then was pulled into the inferno to strengthen the flame. The overcast sky had gone dark grey, bruised with purple and blue. Light flickered through the clouds and I glanced over Ruby's shoulder at Anvil as the exposed skin of my arms prickled.

"Frey," she whispered, not looking away from her barrier.

Her outstretched arms trembled and I placed a hand on the one nearest me. "Let it go, Ruby. Finn needs you."

She swallowed, nodded, and dropped her arms. The fire

remained as she glanced at me, and then fell to nothing when she turned away.

Anvil, Grey, Steed, and Rider stood alongside Chevelle and me atop the ridge. Barrier gone, we could see Rowan calling to the skies. I dared not look for Junnie, who lay at the base of the bank behind us, protecting the child. The wind was cutting without the heat of the flame. And though thunder rolled across the clouds, Rowan's words still reached my ears.

"Kill them. Asher's throne will be yours."

For a moment, I couldn't understand. But then I realized the flicker of light above had not been lightning, but a fey.

"Down," I yelled, rolling from the edge of the ridge onto its slant.

Several shards of solid, toxic ice pierced the earth where we'd been standing, driving through both soil and stone. I glanced up as the attacker dove past and saw dark wings, adorned with flecks the yellow-orange of a monarch butterfly. Suddenly, a burst of power struck and I spun away as rock and dirt exploded beside me. I got to my feet to see Rowan cursing and spitting.

Chevelle and Steed remained on the slope near me, the others spread among the top of the ridge and opposite side. I hoped Junnie was no longer alone.

Chevelle flung a strike at Rowan, but he moved too swiftly and remained unharmed.

Steed eyed the air above us. "So that's the ice boy, eh?"

"Not for long," I answered, narrowing my gaze on the tiny bit of orange visible against the dark clouds.

Before I released a blow, the slim black wings opened and the fairy was diving toward me once more. I hadn't planned on killing him, merely stunning him to the ground to capture and explain Rowan's folly, Asher's madness, so I only allowed a small measure of power into the assault.

When it reached the winged beast, he froze midflight, twisting and writhing, and then jerked against my energy. I believed him to be struggling to overcome the blast, but then Rowan laughed from his vantage point across the charred field and I realized what was happening. I pulled frantically back, trying to draw the energy in, but it was too late. I hadn't thought it possible, hadn't believed this half-blood fey was strong enough. He was stealing my power.

"Take cover," I screamed, severing the tie, and the dark fey beast shrieked a hideous cry.

Steed threw himself against me and Chevelle leapt in front of us both, blocking the debris from the barely missed blast. I gritted my teeth at being knocked once more from the path of destruction so violently, and found my feet again. Rowan used the opportunity to take another shot at me, which infuriated me so severely I sent an excess of power his way. Somehow it missed and a crater appeared in the dirt.

"He's like a snake," I seethed.

Emboldened by his victory, the dark fey floated closer. "She is not so formidable, Rowan." His head tilted to the side as he examined me from the air, purposefully out of reach. "If not for Father's strength, she would be nothing."

"Stop wasting time, Sian," Rowan yelled from his position of safety. "Kill her."

The fey smiled then, and his face changed. He was no boy, but a man. He was slight and thin, but signs of age lined his face. His long black hair was fine and dull, and the papery wings were tattered and fraying.

"Sian," I whispered, wondering if Chevelle knew the meaning of the name.

His palm brushed my back and I knew he did. *The second.*

Asher had planned this all along. Vita had been the first, a unique and powerful light elf, and had borne Aunt Fannie. But he hadn't stopped there. When she'd been a disappointment he'd moved on to the fey. My mother must have been born after those attempts. And maybe he'd even given up on others for a while when she'd shown promise.

But this was Asher's second attempt, and blatantly named as such.

I could see him there, in this fey's eyes, and the resemblance made my stomach turn.

"It doesn't have to end this way," I offered. "You have been misled."

Sian's mouth bent into a smirk. "She is afraid, Rowan. She knows she will die."

Anvil chose that moment to step over the ridge and when Rowan commanded, "End it," the skies came alive with light.

"No," I screamed. But it didn't come in time.

My skin pricked and chest tightened an instant before the deafening crack tore from the sky. Anvil had thrown everything into the attack, and the lightning gathered among the clouds for one long second before threading into several strands that tracked straight for the fey. A blinding flash lit the air around us, followed by an instant of dead silence before the explosion.

Sian had fallen from the sky, but he was far from lifeless. His body thrashed and shook, his chest heaved in a few wicked coughs. And then the screeching sounded again. This time it pierced our ears, strangled at first, but quickly stronger, louder... chilling.

Steed cursed.

I'd no more than began to process what had happened when a large, wet raindrop splatted against my cheek. My head tilted back automatically, and several more landed on my face and chest. I drew in a breath, but Chevelle was already calling out the command.

"Run!"

Suddenly, the air was empty, vacant as Sian drew in the moisture from around us. My feet scrambled for purchase on the slope, now littered with dips and rubble from the conflict, and I looked for the ridge above. The eerie hollowness of the air was intensified by silence, the sudden lack of thunder and wind, and I knew we didn't have long.

Anvil grabbed my arm, pulling me over the ridge, and I caught sight of the trees ahead, lifeless as their leaves had abruptly stilled. I felt the power build and release behind us, but could do nothing to stop it.

Anvil had felt it too, and we were spinning, turning to face the coming onslaught. The others were behind us, and I met Chevelle's eyes for one brief moment before he turned to shield me.

Steel rained down upon us. The ice didn't carry the tang of poison, but it was death. Blades of hardened water shone like glass, flying toward us in an endless assault. We could do nothing to Sian, could not give him more power to use against us, could only watch as he laughed and cackled a scream.

We crouched, huddled together on the edge of the ridge, Steed and Chevelle in front of me, Anvil and Rider at my sides. Grey had disappeared. We blocked every shard we could, but they were razors, cutting the air with no more than a whisper of sound until they pierced the earth around us. Steed flinched as one caught his arm, and another connected with Rider. Blood dampened my cheek an instant before I felt the blade-thin shard brush against it.

Sian raised his arms to the sky and the ice turned to daggers, great crystal spikes in the form of a hailstorm. Anvil was knocked back as a spear took him in the shoulder and then Steed faltered as one planted deep into his leg. Chevelle cursed, trying to pick up the momentary lapse in our shield.

A solid thump rang through my bones before my ears caught the *zzzshk* of a too-close shard and I looked down to find a spear of ice lodged in the side of my chest.

A squeal of delight erupted from the dark fey elf and I glanced up in time to see him dancing in triumph. Numbly, I watched as he spun to a stop and smiled back at me. The ice had stopped too, and the others fell slightly away as they turned to see what had his attention.

Chevelle had gone white. He reached up as if to touch the blade but stopped, instead staring into my eyes. I became very aware of our surroundings, the sudden silence amplifying the chaos. The ridge was destroyed. My guard lay bleeding around me.

Sian would overtake us. Any strike against him would be not only be useless, it would be returned tenfold.

We were hurt. Hopeless.

Finn and Keaton howled from somewhere among the pines.

And then I saw it, there in Chevelle's sapphire eyes. He hadn't given up.

Suddenly, a jolt ran through me. Chevelle hadn't left the blade in my chest because there was no chance. He had left it because I was still breathing. The ice hadn't pierced my lung, but was embedded in the muscle between my chest and shoulder joint. My leather would hold it there, keeping me from further damage, and it wasn't poisoned.

It was, however, the only thing keeping Sian from continuing the attack.

I kept my face slack, letting him think it was shock as I took in the scene. It would be a brief reprieve, regardless, but there had to be some way, some *thing* we could do to fight him.

There was the barest sound from the base of the ridge behind us, some small shifting of stone, and then abruptly a large grey wolf stood beside us. Keaton had bounded onto the demolished earth of the ridge, paws clattering the sharpened ice against stone, and growled toward Sian.

His muzzle was still pulled back in a snarl when he turned to us, but his eyes shone bright. The wolf looked first at Rider, then me. When he was certain he had my attention, he moved his gaze slowly to Chevelle.

I couldn't say how long it took for the message to sink in, but when Keaton finally got through, I nodded. I reached forward to clasp Chevelle's hand.

"The power," I whispered, "hold it for me."

His eyes never left my face as I directed the energy to release. I could feel the line as it stretched within me, as it fell to Chevelle, and as it ran free to its target.

The impact threw Sian off his feet to land soundly in the ash behind him. A puff of dust rose from the destroyed trees and then settled around him as he writhed and moaned. He struggled to control the power, but as he wrapped himself fully around it, the energy would not work free. He let out a high-pitched keen and then his neck snapped up to look at us.

There was no way he could tell, no possibility he would understand, but Sian knew something had changed. He fought to his knees, twitching and jerking, and tried to center his focus.

He pulled harder against it, struggling to wrench the energy free, but it only stretched thinner. Through our connection, I could feel Chevelle now as he anchored the power. I'd had no control over Asher's power alone, but it was steadily fastened within our bond, similar to the way Rhys and Rider had shared it. And our target was growing weaker.

My mouth pulled up in a smile and Sian realized he was no longer assured victory. His face fell, and then his eyes moved along the ridge. I followed his stare to find Junnie, bow raised and drawn in readiness. There was a sharp screech, the call of a bird, and she loosed the arrow.

Junnie didn't wait for it to hit the mark, but jerked her head toward the clearing.

Rowan stood opposite us, watching with horror as the events unfolded. He didn't see the figure slip up behind him, nor the blade, too quick, that sliced his throat. Rowan's hand came up automatically, his blood flooding through the shield of useless fingers.

When he fell, Grey stood behind him.

25

NEW BEGINNINGS

I stared blankly at Grey's lithe form, watching as he drew the dagger across his leg to clean the blade.

"Freya," Chevelle whispered, sliding his hand up to cradle my face, my neck.

My eyes met his and his hand continued to my shoulder, where he squeezed, and I suddenly realized he was bracing me. A choking gasp escaped my throat when Steed pulled the shard free, and then Junnie was there, stitching up the wound.

I blinked, staring up at her, and she smiled in greeting. "Freya."

A long breath fell from me and I sagged as the tension dissipated. We had done it.

"Are we all alive?" I asked, watching Chevelle hold Steed's leg while Anvil removed the hardened ice.

Junnie glared across the field at Rowan's prone form. "The important ones, yes."

Grey was making his way up the slope of the ridge, but detoured to check on Sian's body. Junnie's arrow had pierced the dark fey's heart.

"There," Junnie said as she patted my shoulder. "The wounds are clean. The blades were thin and sharp, so the cuts fall right together and, once sealed"—she glanced at Steed's leg—"will heal well in time."

Grey kicked a shard of ice as he approached, appearing completely unscathed. Rowan had been slippery, but he'd met his match here. He smiled as Ruby came to join us.

"How is Finn?" Rider asked as he took his turn at Junnie's hand.

Ruby smirked. "He's the best patient I've ever had." She eyed the lot of us, bruised and bloody, and the mirth dropped from her expression. "He's had it the worst," she explained, "because of the poison." She shrugged. "But, lucky for us, Frey was attacked weeks ago and I've had some time to study the toxin."

"Yeah," I muttered. "Lucky."

She smiled down at me. "He'll be fine."

Anvil passed me a canteen and I drank deep. I would have thought I'd have been done with water for a while, but I couldn't seem to get enough of it. Eventually, the others gathered in the pines with Rhys and Finn as we prepared to return to the castle. I remained on the ridge with Junnie, where she cradled a small, half-human child.

"Junnie," I asked, sliding the pendant from my belt, "what do you know of this?"

Her eyes narrowed on Veil's gift, and I explained his visit and our theory in more detail.

She nodded. "That's four. The ice and silver you know." Her gaze came up to mine. "And bone," she said. "Freya, that's you."

"What?" I argued. "Why would I be a danger to myself?"

Junnie shook her head. "It wasn't a warning for you, Freya. It was the four who could claim the throne."

"But Asher had more," I contended. "There were so many."

"Yes," she agreed. "But not all of them were capable of ascending the throne."

I sighed. "Then who is the fourth?"

Her eyes stayed on me a long moment, too long, and then we both looked at the child in her arms.

"No," I moaned.

"Blood," Junnie answered levelly. "She is of the blood, Frey. Half human and Asher's own child."

Half human. *Like me.*

Rowan had burned these woods to find Asher's baby. Junnie had risked her own life to save her.

And now Junnie's bright blue eyes peered into mine. Beseeching, daring me, I didn't know. But I could feel the child, the slightest brush of her mind, and I knew she would live.

When she saw the change in me, Junnie's posture relaxed, and it was only then I realized she'd not wanted to fight either. She'd not wanted it to be me any more than I'd wanted it to be her.

"Ah, Junnie," I sighed, "there's more."

Once I'd explained my bargain with Veil, Junnie and I said goodbye to go our separate ways. She, with the child, would set the new Council into power and restructure the south. And I, with my guard, would rule the north.

"Are you well?" Chevelle asked as he helped me onto my horse.

My brows furrowed. "Yes, I guess I am."

He shook his head at my answer before climbing onto his own mount, and we kicked them up to where the others waited.

It was a long ride home beneath the graying skies. Finn had been secured atop a horse, Keaton running beside them. Anvil's previously injured shoulder had been sliced through and patched up so that he tilted in the saddle. Ruby looked tired, but refused to give in, and Chevelle had received more cuts than he'd let on.

I had too much time to think.

When we finally made it home, it was late the following afternoon. The eight of us slid stiff and wobbly off the horses, staggering numbly through the stable-side entry. There were a few reports, a couple of called-out orders, and one angry mountain lion before I at last found a bath. I soaked for an endless hour, possibly dozing off once or twice, and then slid into a clean, fresh dressing gown.

After tying a loose robe over that, I stretched my arms to test the movement. Junnie had been right. It was tender, but there didn't seem to be any real damage done.

When I opened my door, I glanced down the hallways to be certain the corridor was empty.

My bare feet slapped lightly against the cool stone as I ran, heading to my favorite perch. I passed two doorways and then turned, suddenly abandoning the plan. It was not where I wanted to be.

I stood before his door for a long moment, staring at the wooded planks. When I finally pushed it open, I saw his silhouette against the filigreed window. Sliding the door shut behind me, I walked slowly across the room. My arms wrapped around his chest, cheek pressed firmly against his back as he stared out the window.

He took a deep breath and rested his hand over mine.

As we stood together, my eye caught the glint of a chipped basin on the corner table, and I smiled.

At first, his room appeared sparse, as if he'd never intended to stay. But now I realized everything had a memory attached to it. The basin I'd broken as a child. The blanket he'd hidden when I'd accidentally caught my room on fire and scorched it. The sword his mother had given him when we'd snuck out to meet her.

"What is it?" Chevelle asked as he turned to hold me in his arms.

"I was just thinking," I lied, "that we should move into the main suites. Now that we are bound." My head tilted briefly to the side. "If you can give up this view, that is."

He stared down at me, window forgotten, and the corner of his mouth pulled up in a slow smile. "I quite prefer another view."

I laid my hand on his chest, over the beat of his heart, and he leaned down. His lips brushed softly over mine.

The kiss was sweet, slow. It said we had time.

It said we had forever.

The next day, I sat kneeling in front of my bureau. It had been my first real night with Chevelle, and I'd woken refreshed, my dreams no longer haunted by flame. My issues, if temporarily, had been laid to rest.

The fey had been watching us for a long time, maybe guiding things to their own advantage. But for now, I felt safe. We had the north, and Junnie's new Council the south. We had balanced the power, so there was no need for war. But if Veil were pushed, if the fey struck, together we could overcome them.

"You have almost nothing of interest in here," Ruby complained from the wardrobe behind me.

"Well," I answered, not looking away from my task, "then it should be easy to move."

Ruby laughed, but I did, in truth, have plenty of interest here. I thought of the box, hidden beneath the stone floor below the bed.

It was time to start a new life, new memories. The others would stay buried within the box, as they should be.

"I still have some things to work out," Ruby murmured. "But at least I know where the wolves were all that time."

I slid the bureau drawer shut and stacked the filled box with the others.

"Like these," Ruby continued, walking over to hand me a small slip of paper.

I turned, taking one last, long look out my window.

Fellon Strago Dreg.

Even Chevelle had not known the meaning when he'd used the message so long ago. He'd simply seen the opportunity and taken it.

"So," Ruby reminded me. "What's it mean?"

I glanced down at the message, written in my mother's hand.

The warning had followed me, questioned my every move. And it was still here now, in the midst of so much rightness. As I had accepted my place under the weight of the throne.

I couldn't help the sardonic smile that crossed my lips before I answered her question.

"Nothing as it seems, Ruby. Nothing as it seems."

MORE FROM
MELISSA WRIGHT

THE FREY SAGA
Frey
Pieces of Eight
Molly (a short story)
Rise of the Seven
Venom and Steel

DESCENDANTS SERIES
Bound by Prophecy
Shifting Fate
Reign of Shadows

SHATTERED REALMS
King of Ash and Bone

Visit the Author on the web at
www.melissa-wright.com

Please look for book four in the Frey Saga:

VENOM AND STEEL

26996705R00133

Made in the USA
San Bernardino, CA
24 February 2019